# Treading Water

Belle A. DeCosta

Sherri, - Always face the sun!
Belle A DeCosta

**Treading Water.**



Produced and printed
by Stillwater River Publications.



Visit our website at
www.StillwaterPress.com
for more information.
First Stillwater River Publications Edition
Library of Congress Control Number: 2021923153
ISBN: 978-1-955123-65-5
1 2 3 4 5 6 7 8 9 10
Written by Belle A. DeCosta.
Published by Stillwater River Publications,
Pawtucket, RI, USA.

*For my grandson Ian and his beautiful mother.*

*My whole heart, always.*

# Treading Water

# Chapter I

The drum pounding in her head brought Caroline out of sleep and into a hangover stupor. *When will you ever learn*? she berated herself. Swinging her legs over the side of the bed, she sat up and groaned as the drum became a full-fledged band marching inside her skull. Reaching for the water bottle on the nightstand, nausea overtook her as the bed shifted and a pair of hands landed on her waist. "Crap – looks like I went for the full Monty last night," she mumbled, batting his hands away. Undeterred, he reached for her again.

"Last night's invitation didn't include breakfast," she croaked and, with her back still to him, ordered him out. She heard a male voice growl "Bitch," followed by the rustling sounds of someone dressing and the slam of the front door.

Caroline didn't remember his name (if she had ever known it), couldn't say what he looked like; if he was young or old, wealthy, or homeless. Nor did she care. She had learned from experience it was easier to maintain a warped sense of self-dignity when you thought of the men as non-entities. They were no more than a coping mechanism, much like but not nearly as important as her best friend, Don Julio.

At the thought of tequila, her body kicked into its now-familiar routine. Stumbling to the bathroom, Caroline emptied her stomach into the toilet, then forced herself into an ice-cold shower. After the pulsating sleet had her feeling almost alive, she toweled off and went to make coffee strong enough to do the same for her brain.

She was made-up, coiffed, dressed to the nines, and almost ready to roll within the hour, looking infinitely more put together than she felt, which wasn't saying much. Caroline called down to have her car brought around, rid her stomach of the two cups of coffee and four aspirins she'd consumed, brushed her teeth, applied lipstick, slid into her Jimmy Choos, and was out the door. By the time the elevator reached the foyer, she had donned her game-face and sunglasses. The doorman, seeing her stride towards him, held the door open with a cheery "Good morning, Ms. McMerritt."

"Is it Robert?" she asked, brushing past him into her waiting car. Caroline was glad to see the glass partition in place. The last thing she wanted was inane chit-chat with a person she had no interest in knowing. What she did desperately need was a cigarette but knew better than to light up, having lost two drivers due to her bad habit. It was beyond her why it was illegal to smoke in a private vehicle because an employee was present but had finally complied. Maci informed her if she kept costing the firm drivers and fines, they would pull her car.

Maci. As much as Caroline hated to admit it, the little witch was a brilliant ad exec and had recently managed to make partner ahead of her. Caroline, the firm's top moneymaker for nine of the last ten years, assumed Maci had cut her in line by laying on her back. What other explanation was there? It was Caroline who had an A list of clients who would only work with her – one of whom she was going to be late meeting if Brad, or Brett, or whoever, didn't break free from the tangled traffic. *One job. He's got one job and can't handle it,* she angrily thought. Lowering the glass partition, she snarled, "Let me out here; I'll have to walk the rest of the way."

"Ms. McMerritt, I can't control the traf–." She slammed the door mid-sentence, narrowly missing the “Bitch” hurled at her for the second time that morning, and joined the sea of pedestrians. The incompetent little twerp had cost her the only chance at a smoke until lunchtime.

Finally reaching her building, a revolving door deposited her into a vast marble-floored lobby. Caroline ran as fast as her four-inch spikes allowed, shoved her way onto a crowded elevator, and pushed number twenty-five. She had to mouth-breath to prevent the toxic mixture of colognes and perfumes from further upsetting her stomach.

The advertising firm, Perkins, Galvin, and Galvin, founded by two brothers and a friend at the end of WWII, grew from a basement office in the Bronx to an international company. PG&G's New York headquarters occupied the entire twenty-fifth floor of Manhattan's most prestigious office building. It was the premier job to land for anyone trying to claw their way to the top of the advertising world. If you were obsessed, driven, and made the firm your only priority, you had a place at PG&G; anything less, you were out. It was a dream come true for a young, ambitious Caroline years ago and was still the center of her world.

Pushing her way out of the elevator, she raced down the hallway of cubicles, ignoring all the "Good mornings" sent her way. Breezing into her personal outer office, she barked at her assistant, Hector, to bring her a bottle of water and a cup of coffee stat. Once in her private domain, Caroline threw her coat and briefcase on the couch and sat down behind a humungous glass top desk to catch her breath. She swiveled to face the panoramic view her corner office awarded her, grateful that her first appointment was running late. Seconds later, impatient as always, she turned to push the intercom button to summon Hector and caught him leaning against the door-jam observing her. At five foot three and 125 pounds, the short, dark, handsome metrosexual could pack a judgment punch bigger than someone twice his size.

"You can wipe that tsk-tsk motherly look off your face," she snapped. "And where's my coffee?"

"You need a helluva lot more than coffee to pull that look together this morning," he said sarcastically.

"Talk like that will get you fired."

"You can't fire me; I'm married to your brother. Besides, you love me," he said with a dismissive wave.

"I will do my bloody best to change both those things if you do not bring me coffee NOW!"

"You don't have time. Maci wants to see you in her office immediately."

"Tell her I can't; I'm expecting the Wagner account any minute." *Thank God!* Maci was the last thing she needed right now.

Hector softened his tone. "Wagner's CEO called first thing this morning to cancel, then asked to be put through to Maci."

Knowing full well what that meant, Caroline looked at him dumbfounded. The Wagner account was her baby. She was the one who wooed them over to PG&G, and they had enjoyed a stellar relationship for years. Why would they want to switch account execs now?

As Caroline made her way to Maci's office, she decided some young hotshot must've schmoozed them behind her back and won them over. Well, she'd put a quick end to that. Nobody stole Caroline McMerritt's clients and lived to talk about it. Whoever it was, she would ruin them professionally.

Ready to do battle, she stormed past Maci's assistant and entered her private office, ranting, "Who is it? I want a name! They are done in this business!" *What the hell...* she pulled up short when she saw Phillip, Wagner's CEO, sitting across from Maci. Before she could greet him, he stood, shook Maci's hand, and walked past Caroline as if she was invisible.

"Sit down, Caroline." It was a demand, not a request. Maci walked around her desk to take the position of power and waited for Caroline to be seated. Knowing how the game was played, Caroline remained standing. Brash, over six feet tall in heels, with long auburn curls as unruly as she, and fierce green eyes burning with confidence, Caroline always cut an imposing figure. But standing with her feet firmly planted, chin in the air, and barely controlled anger seeping through her pores, she was downright intimidating.

Maci was unaffected. "Suit yourself, then," she said and sat down behind her desk.

Petite, blonde, and blue-eyed, Maci looked like she should be cheerleading on a college campus. Until you felt her presence. She never raised her voice or lost her composure, and her unwavering eye contact and air of intelligence sliced through the best of them. She could smell bullshit a mile away and feared nothing and no one.

"I want to know who stole the Wagner account!" Caroline demanded.

"No one," Maci replied, "you lost it all on your own."

"Do you honestly expect me to believe that after all the years Phillip has been singing my praises?" Caroline fumed.

"I didn't hear him sing to you just now, did you?" Maci had her there. "Caroline, you know better than anyone how cut-throat this business is and how unforgiving clients are. Reputation carries you only as far as your first ball drop. You've managed to hold on longer than most, but it's caught up to you."

Caroline choked out a laugh. "You're honestly trying to tell me I'm off my game?"

"No, Caroline, I'm not. Your clients are. Phillip isn't the only complaint I've gotten about your work this past year."

*Clients going over my head and not being straight with me? No, no way.* The thought wouldn't even settle in her mind.

"If that's the case, why are you just telling me now? There's no love lost between us. It's not like you would cover for me. No, there's something else going on, and I want to know what it is. Right now."

Maci folded her hands on the desk, looked Caroline straight in the eye, and let her have it.

"You have a drinking problem, Caroline, and burning the candle at both ends has caught up with you. You're in a fog until noon, miss meetings, and drink too much at client dinners. You haven't landed a new client or come up with a decent concept in almost a year. Before the firm acted, we needed to have documented proof it was affecting your work."

Caroline's already compromised stomach lurched. "You're getting rid of me? Well, don't think I'm going quietly—."

Macy cut her off. "If it were up to me, you'd be gone, but the board's not ready to cut you loose. Yet. Take the summer off, get some help, and dry out. You're in trouble, Caroline. You're headed down a slippery slope physically and emotionally. Use the summer wisely and save yourself; you're the only one who can."

Enraged, Caroline slammed both hands down on Maci's desk and leaned into her personal space. "And if I refuse?"

Maci never flinched. "Then you can clean out your desk and be escorted out of the building now. Those are your only two options."

"I've given everything to this firm, not to mention made it some serious money, and this is how I'm rewarded?" Caroline railed.

"This *is* a reward; anyone else would have been fired months ago. Oh, and Caroline, your leave begins immediately."

And with that, Maci ended the meeting.

# Chapter II

Blind with fury, Caroline stormed back to her office, slammed the door, and lit a cigarette. She was savvy enough to know her career probably wouldn't survive four months out of the rat race and knew her psyche wouldn't either. PG&G was her life; it was all she had left now that Jack was gone. Caroline had sacrificed everything for the firm and was not going down without a fight. She vowed to make her absence as painful as possible for the company.

Hector entered, unannounced, and answered his boss's glare with, "You wouldn't have let me in had I knocked."

"Exactly. So get out," Caroline growled.

Ignoring her, he took the cigarette, ran it under water, and threw it in the trash. "You know better than to smoke in here," he scolded.

"What are they going to do, fire me?"

"Rumor has it, that's a substantial possibility." Caroline looked at him, mortified the entire office already knew.

Hector shrugged, "Word travels fast, especially a tidbit this juicy. Come on, let's get you out of here."

He collected her coat and bag and, trying to eliminate some of the sting, swept his hand out in a noble gesture to escort her to the door. "Your chariot awaits curbside, my Queen." Unamused, she slapped his hand away, and he sobered. "I know time off is inconceivable to you, but trust me, as someone who loves you, it needs to happen. You've been slowly self-destructing since Jack left, and the behavior is accelerating. You're going to implode if you don't stop. Please, use this time to heal."

Glaring, Caroline swiped her belongings from him and, with head held high, stormed out of the office and out of the building. Once in the car, she pulled out a cigarette, her palpable fury enough to stop the driver from complaining. *That sanctimonious little bitch Maci, who does she think she is?* Caroline tried to light up but found her hands trembling too hard to get the job done. Being honest with herself, she knew the tremors weren't all due to anger; she was also terrified. Since her college internship at the firm, PG&G had been her center, her focus. At thirty-five, the thought of her lifeline yanked away, even temporarily, left her in a free fall.

*Will! He'll know what to do.* The thought of her big brother calmed Caroline down considerably. Four years her senior, Will had protected her from the day she was born, mostly from herself. Where Caroline was the epitome of impulsive, hot-headed rashness, Will exuded an air of thoughtful, calm, even-temperedness. Caroline screamed through life while Will ambled along with quiet reason. He balanced her, the Yin to her Yang. She adored him and trusted him unconditionally. He'd know how to fix this mess. Feeling better about things, she gave the driver Will's address and sat back for the long commute to Risedale, Connecticut.

The town of Risedale, a compromise for Will and Hector, satisfied both their needs. Nestled in the foothills of the Berkshire Mountains, it had a quaint small-town feel. Restored Victorian homes stood majestically along tree-lined streets leading to lush parks and hiking trails. Horse farms shared winding roads with mini-mansions built by commuters eager to raise their families out of NYC. The mixture of artists, horse breeders, and suburbanites gave the town an eclectic atmosphere, making it a good fit for Will. As for Hector, Risedale's biggest draws were Will and its location – less than sixty miles from Manhattan. Unlike Will, Hector, born and raised in NYC, thrived on the fast-paced, cultural melting pot he grew up in. The rudeness, grime, and overpopulation Will groused about was part of the Big Apple's charm to Hector. Whenever he started jonesing, as Will fondly called it, Hector stayed in the city at Caroline's for a night or two to get his fix of nightlife and craziness. Will was flannel shirts and earthy, Hector all about fashion and flashy, much like their personalities. The couple was proof positive opposites attract, and the combination left many people shaking their heads. But they clicked the moment they met in Caroline's office five years ago and have defied the odds ever since.

As the car passed through Main Street, a menagerie of cafes, shops, and art galleries, Caroline quickly checked her lipstick and popped a breath mint. Will hated the fact that she was smoking again, and she wasn't up for a lecture today. The driver turned into the dirt road that served as Will's driveway, and Caroline was struck as she always was by the beauty of her brother's property. Endless horse pastures stretched in front of a sprawling, clapboard farmhouse elegantly dressed in a wrap-around porch. Behind the house sat a barn, now converted into a studio, where Will worked his magic. Beyond that, endless fields spread out like finely woven carpets laid at the feet of the rolling hills. Will had bought the dilapidated property for a song and, with his own hands, restored it to its original grandeur.

While Caroline could appreciate the Norman Rockwell setting, she didn't understand the lifestyle. Why would anyone want to be so far from the action, so disengaged? And why on earth live without all the city had to offer at your fingertips? Sometimes she wondered how they came from the same gene pool. Still pondering that thought, she stepped out of the car into ankle-deep mud that promptly devoured one of her $600 shoes. "Goddammit!" she yelled. Trying to hide his smirk, the driver helped her pull her foot out and tipped his cap in farewell.

"Where do you think you're going?" she asked, aiming her anger at him.

"I was instructed to drop you at your destination and return immediately," he said.

"They're suspending my car service?"

"Apparently, ma'am," he said, getting into the car.

"You could have told me that before I had you drive me two hours out of the city!"

"I thought you knew," he shrugged and pulled away. Caroline saw him smile in the rearview. She could imagine his thoughts, the way he was thinking he owed her this for always smoking in his car and treating him like gum on her shoe – *like he didn't deserve it.* As she watched him turn the corner at the end of the drive, she swore he was laughing.

Livid, Caroline flung her mud-caked shoe at the retreating car and sat down on the porch steps. Could this day possibly get any worse? She didn't see how. Craving a drink or five, she took off her other shoe and barefoot, trudged through the mud towards the studio and her hero who would save the day.

# Chapter III

Caroline paused in the studio doorway to admire her brother at work. Tall, over six foot two, Will had the muscular, solid body of a man not afraid of physical labor. His rough hands, calloused from years of woodworking, were also capable of the intricate finish work that set his pieces apart. The unique cabinetry and custom furniture he created were works of art and well-renowned.

Where Caroline had inherited her father's looks, Will favored their mother. Black curls, always needing a trim, rested on his collar, and a prominent nose and chin gave him an air of Gaelic pride. But Will's most striking feature, by far, were his eyes. Deep liquid pools of blue, they possessed a hypnotic effect. They danced when amused, shone with a keen perceptiveness, were framed by lashes women would kill for, and they held an underlying hint of vulnerability. Will had always been, and still was, oblivious to his commanding presence and good looks. Which, of course, only added to his charisma. He had unwittingly broken many a heart, both male and female, over the years.

Will shut the lathe down and turned to find his sister at the door. "You don't look surprised to see me," she said. "Let me guess: Hector called."

Will shrugged. "He said you'd probably be coming by, that you'd had a rough morning."

"Rough? More like brutal. But those bastards aren't going beat me," she said. Hearing the slight quiver in her voice, Will planted a kiss atop her head, draped his arm around her shoulder, and led her back to the house.

While Will made coffee, Caroline filled him in on her meeting with Maci verbatim. Expecting her brother to match her indignation and rise to her defense, she was surprised when he just poured their coffee and sat down. "Well?" she asked.

"I think that's more than fair," he said.

Caroline immediately laced up her emotional boxing gloves. "Fair?! Did you even listen to me?"

"I heard every word, sis. I always do. I think they make a valid point."

Caroline started to panic. *Will? Even Will was against her?* As if reading her mind, he gently said, "No one is against you, Caroline. We're trying to help you. You're drowning in more ways than one."

Caroline tried to bite off an indignant retort, but her brother's eyes were boring through her façade and deep into her truth. Will held her gaze until he was sure he had penetrated her armored shell and reached the essence of the sister he knew. When he finally spoke, Caroline was surprised to taste the salt of her tears. "You need to take time to go within to clear your head and heal your heart. You can't hide behind tequila and empty sex any longer, sis. Your vices aren't protecting you; they are overtaking you."

Caroline's insides turned to liquid. "Oh my God! Are you suggesting rehab? I DO NOT need rehab, and there is no way I'll sign in –"

Will cut her off, "I didn't say rehab; I said some time away to regroup." That somewhat calmed Caroline down, and she managed to find her snark.

"What a smashing idea, darling," she cooed as she started to sashay around the kitchen. "Perhaps the south of France? Or maybe the Amalfi Coast in Italy? I hear Bora Bora is magnificent."

"Knock it off, Caroline. This is real," Will scolded and fixed her with a withering stare.

Chastised, she plopped down in a chair and waited. She knew her brother well enough to know he had already figured out what was best for her and had a plan.

"You should go to the cabin in Maine."

"The cabin? Surely, you jest," she said, not trying to hide her distaste. "I'd rather go to hell. Anyway, I thought you sold it after Mom and Dad died."

"They were so fond of the place, it felt like a betrayal to their memory, so I kept it."

The cabin was their family vacation home where they'd spent summers growing up. Long, hot, bug-infested, poison ivy-filled, dull summers that Will always loved and Caroline tolerated. Sure, it was fun as a kid, but she would long to get back to Connecticut and civilization once a teenager. "Will, that's your thing, not mine. There is nothing for me to do there; I'll go crazy!"

"You're already crazy, and there is plenty to do." He softened it with a wink. "Hiking, canoeing, biking, gardening, swimming, reading, meditation…" Caroline stopped him by blocking her ears and singing *Lalala* at the top of her lungs.

"Mature, very classy," he said behind a grin.

Ignoring him, she continued her tirade. "When have you ever seen me do any of those things as an adult, much less enjoy them? What the hell would I even wear? Jimmy Choo doesn't make hiking boots. And dig in the dirt? Do you know what I spend on these nails? Peddle a bike? Sweat? I don't even own a bathing suit that's ever been wet. Meditate? Seriously? You're the one that's lost their mind!"

Will just stood, arms crossed, with a half-smile, listening to his sister rant. He learned long ago not to try to reason with her until her fire turned to embers. When she finally came up for air, he said the only words he knew for sure would make her go.

"Do it for me." He had her.

Will dropped her off at the commuter rail and said he'd pick her up in the city in a couple of days after she'd packed, and he completed a piece he was working on.

Two days later, Caroline found herself riding shotgun in Will's Jeep Cherokee on her way to Maine, asking herself how in the world she'd let this happen. A rhetorical question since she already knew the answer, never having been able to deny Will anything. A fact that aggravated her to no end at times like this. "You didn't play fair," she pouted.

"It's tough to win against you when playing fair, and this was too important to chance a loss."

*Touché bro,* Caroline thought. "How is it you always manage to stay in my good graces even when I hate you?" she pouted.

"Must be my charm."

Caroline flipped him her middle finger. "That's what I think of you and your charm right now."

Will laughed and blew her a kiss, throwing gas on her fire. Seeing her face turn as red as her hair, he reached over and cranked up the radio, assuming, from past experiences, a raging tirade was about to happen. It didn't. She couldn't rage, not with the fear churning around inside of her. *I'm going to be alone with my thoughts and no distractions, What will I discover, what truths will I have to face?* She was terrified of going within. It didn't occur to her Will had to have taken a similar journey to arrive at his truth, self-acceptance and peace.

"It's going to be okay, sis, not easy, but okay. You don't have to be afraid," Will said, as if knowing what she was thinking.

That got her going. Even if Caroline was scared, she would never let other people see it, not even Will. "Afraid? When have I ever been afraid of anything you twit? What I'll be is sober, horny, bored, pissed, and counting down the days to freedom!" Her bravado wasn't fooling either one of them, but Will let it go.

To fill the silence, Will tuned in to Steely Dan while Caroline stewed in her thoughts. The further they drove into the wilderness, the more apprehensive she got. *Seriously, what am I going to do out here?* She remembered the so-called town of Addisen nestled on a lake, consisting of a general store, gas station, laundromat, and a bait shop. Traveling clockwise around the lake were seasonal campgrounds, rental cabins, and an overnight camp for kids who stayed anywhere from a week to the entire summer. The south shore, mostly private chalets owned by avid fishermen and seasonal hunters, was followed by family-owned vacation homes, some passed down through generations. Those properties usually had hammocks, fire pits, various bird feeders, and gardens. The closest thing to civilization was at least twenty miles away, a draw for everyone but Caroline. Even as a kid, she hated feeling disconnected from the action.

"Ugh" was the first sound she'd uttered in over two hours as they passed by the "Welcome to Addisen Lake" sign. After an eternity of driving on a dusty dirt road full of potholes, Will pulled into the overgrown yard of their cabin. "Nice family estate," Caroline groaned.

"No one's been up here for quite some time. It looks like you'll have something to keep you busy after all," Will quipped.

Caroline shot him a glare and opened the cabin door. To her surprise and relief, the place was spotless. The surfaces and floors in the combined living/kitchen area were scrubbed clean, curtains and linens freshly washed, and the braided throw rugs dust-free. A bowl of fresh fruit sat on the table, and a vase of wildflowers dressed the mantle. A basket of firewood sat next to the hearth, completing the cozy atmosphere. A quick peek into the main bedroom and bath showcased the same results, so she assumed the loft area was pristine as well. Will saw his sister's puzzled look. "The camp counselors have to report two weeks before the campers, so I hired a couple of them to clean the place." Caroline begrudgingly shot him a "Thanks" over her shoulder and headed out to start unloading the car. The quicker they unpacked, the sooner she could send Will on his way and have a drink.

Within the hour, they'd emptied the Jeep Cherokee, and Will was ready to go. He gave her a hug, cuffed her under her chin like she was a little girl, and lumbered towards his Jeep. Before backing out, he lowered the window. "Oh, before I go… the bottles of tequila you hid under sheets and towels didn't make the trip. The linens are in the pink tote bag."

"I hate you, Will McMerritt!" Caroline charged the Jeep Cherokee like a raging bull. He waved and beeped the horn as he pulled away, tears filling his eyes.

*How dare he?* She hurled a couple of rocks after the retreating Jeep and stormed into the cabin. Now she'd have to go into town. They wouldn't have top-shelf tequila, but at this point, anything would do. Remembering the family had kept an old truck at the lake, she went to retrieve the keys in the desk drawer. She found a note instead.

*Hi Sis,*

*Sorry, but I took the truck keys with me to prevent you from going on the lamb. The bicycles and moped are in the boat shed and will get you to and from the general store for supplies. Please get well.*

*I love you, Will*

"Well, doesn't this day just keep getting better and better," Caroline lamented to no one.

# Chapter IV

Never one to exercise, Caroline chose to take the moped and headed out to the boat shed. In her haste to get going, she didn't see the spider web encasing the doorway and plowed into it. Disgusted and swatting at the silk threads clinging to her face, her scream of "God, I want a drink" echoed through the metal shed. Grumbling, she started the moped and took off in the wrong direction, thanks to her mounting stress. Circling three-quarters of the lake to get to town only added to her foul mood.

By the time she got to the store, her nerves were tingling on high alert and her mind was nothing more than jagged edges. She and her bad-temper tore into the store, but one look behind the counter pulled her up short. Bent over was a perfectly shaped male buttock tightly encased in a pair of jeans looking equal to, if not yummier, than Bruce Springsteen's. Thinking there might be some hope for the summer yet, and still admiring the view, Caroline coquettishly leaned on the counter and said, "Excuse me."

Things only improved when he stood. She was gazing upon the very definition of ruggedly handsome. He had a magnificent body, the kind born naturally from physical labor, topped by a stubbled square jaw, sun-kissed skin, and unruly wavy hair. It all complimented his perfect ass quite nicely.

"Can I help you?" He asked.

*Oh, you so can and will,* she thought, but aloud said only, "Point me in the direction of your liquor aisle, please."

"Sorry, I can't. We don't have one. Addisen is a dry town."

Caroline couldn't believe what she was hearing. "You mean people come up to this God-forsaken place and don't drink?"

He chuckled. "I didn't say that. They bring plenty of their own."

*God damn Will!* He knew this, she was sure. *Well, there's always plan B.*

"Undoubtedly, you have a cache of your own. Couldn't you sell me a bottle or two?" She asked with a wink.

"Sorry, I don't drink. And even if I did, I couldn't sell it to you. I own this store, and it would be illegal."

With her humor gone, her flirtatious attitude fizzled, and Caroline slammed out of the store. As if she wasn't frustrated enough, the old moped refused to start. She growled, dropped it to the ground, and gave it a couple of sounding kicks, unaware that Ruggedly Handsome had followed her. Caroline jumped when he cleared his throat. "It's probably out of gas. I'll walk it over to the gas station and fill it up for you. You should keep a spare can on hand."

In her haste to get a drink, she hadn't bothered to check the tank. "Thanks," she managed as she hobbled beside him towards the gas station.

"Your foot hurt?"

"No!" She snapped.

He gave her an amused smile. "I'm Dan, by the way, Dan Preace. And you are?"

"Caroline McMerritt. My family used to summer here."

Dan stopped short and gave her a peculiar look. "You're Will McMerritt's kid sister." It was a statement, not a question.

"Yes, though no one's called me that in years. I take it you know Will?" she asked.

"Will and I were camp counselors together during our high school summers; we were pretty close for a while." With a deep breath, Dan suddenly snapped back to the present and added, "That was a lifetime ago. I haven't seen him in years. How's he doing?"

Caroline told him where her brother lived, about his successful business, and his reputation as a woodworker. She mentioned he was married but left out his partner's name. Will had always been open about being gay with the family, but she wasn't sure when he had come out to his friends. Dan started the moped for her. "Well, glad to hear he's in a good place. Take care, and I'm sure we'll run into each other again."

"Oh, you can count on it," Caroline all but purred with a wave. Even in her pissed off agitated state, her default setting was one of seduction.

Back home, she parked the moped in the shed and allowed all her frustration and anger to take over. Barging through the cabin door, she paced around like a caged animal. *What am I going to do? I'll go crazy sober here all summer! Clients going behind my back, PG&G forcing me to take a leave, Will exiling me to the wilderness? Control freaks, one and all!* "Who the hell do they think they are?!" she bellowed.

Caroline was getting ready to throw something when a thought occurred to her. Their parents used to have a cocktail before dinner. There must be alcohol left somewhere in the cabin. With a feeling of hope, she started tearing through closets and cupboards, growing more frantic as each one came up empty. When she found the last cupboard bare, Caroline had a complete meltdown. She'd grown accustomed to an underlying layer of anger in the past year, but this was an uncontrollable rage. She hated everyone and everything, including herself. Especially herself. She screamed her voice to silence, sobbed long after her tears were dry, and pummeled the floor with her fists, trying to relieve her inner torment. Finally, with her energy spent and emotionally exhausted, she laid there for what felt like an eternity.

Watching her bruised and bloody hands shake and choking on the bile as it rose in her throat, Caroline was forced to admit she was the one with the control problem. She didn't have any. They were right – she was in trouble.

# Chapter V

Caroline pulled herself up onto trembling legs. She spotted her mother's old rocker in front of the fireplace and a wave of nostalgia washed over her. Her mom spent many a night in that chair reading or knitting. She hadn't realized the comfort that vision had provided her in childhood, the immense feeling of protection and love, until this very moment. She cocooned herself in the crocheted afghan folded on the back of the chair and began rocking gently. Immediately she felt her mom's presence surround her, and she began to cry again. *Oh, Mom, I've really done it this time. Please stay with me. I need your strength, your guidance.* It was the first time as an adult Caroline ever remembered asking for help.

Emotionally spent and soothed by her mother's presence, she drifted off to sleep, waking to total darkness as the mantle clock chimed four o'clock. When she turned on the reading lamp, a bolt of lightning shot through her pupils, accompanied by unrelenting thunder pounding in her temples. Caroline quickly shut it off, gagging on the rancid smell of her sweat-soaked clothes. Shaking badly, she made her way to the bathroom and forced herself into a cold shower. Feeling somewhat stronger and less clammy, Caroline toweled off and threw on a tee shirt and sweats. Too twitchy to sleep and too nauseous to eat, she wrapped herself in the afghan and went out to sit on the porch. Swaying on the porch swing, lost in a fog of despair and withdrawal, she was oblivious to the beauty of her surroundings, so peaceful and undisturbed. The reflection of the moonlight as played on the lake. The majestic dark pines, standing tall and proud as they guarded the lake's perimeter. The gentle sound of water lapping as it kissed the shore. Birds started to wake, singing their various songs while crickets chirped backup vocals. Nature was trying its best to calm her, pull her out of herself, but she was blind to it all. Every time Caroline was still, thoughts of Jack and feelings of regret and shame took over, and peace was nothing more than an elusive shadow. As was her habit, Caroline met it with impatient anger, directed at herself. *Let it go, woman! What's done is done.* It was at this point she invariably poured a drink or buried herself in work. Because she could do neither, she stomped in circles shrieking to the heavens, ending not only her efforts but nature's as well. Everything went silent, save the tortured voice in her head.

Caroline made breakfast to distract herself, but the sight of eggs made her gag, the toast got stuck in her throat, and the coffee poured into her already sour stomach made her heave. She tried to read, but her mind wouldn't focus, and it felt like ants were crawling on her skin. There was nothing to clean or unpack, so she went back outside and took a couple of deep breaths as panic set in. *Christ, if this is how your body reacts to not drinking, it's a wonder anyone ever quits.* Thinking a cigarette might settle her nerves, she went inside to find a pack then headed down to the water. Lighting up, she eagerly waited for the rush of nicotine to work its magic. Instead, her body revolted, and she felt even more ill than before. She dropped to her knees and, with her arms around her stomach, began to rock. No work, no city, no alcohol, no cigarettes, and worst of all, no diversions. *Oh God, no distractions… I can't do this! I. Give. Up.* Caving in under pressure wasn't something she'd ever done before, but then she had never been up against herself. With her strength drained, she folded. Caroline went to bed and stayed there.

*Have I been here days? Weeks? By the smell of things, months. Am I dead? No, I'm thirsty. Dead people don't get thirsty, do they? Should I open my eyes? Will that horrendous pain shoot through my head again? My stomach isn't heaving, and my shaking seems to have subsided. Both are good signs, aren't they? Jesus, I've only been a drunk for a year. What do lifers go through? I am a drunk!* That admission brought Caroline back to the land of the living. She opened her eyes and was relieved to feel the searing pain in her head had dulled to an ache. Gingerly, she made her way to the bathroom and drank from the faucet. She couldn't remember ever being so dehydrated. After drinking what felt like gallons of water, she stood and looked at herself in the mirror. "I am a drunk," she said out loud. "I. Am. A. Drunk.," she repeated, louder this time. Her body was through the worst of its recovery, and now the rest was up to her. The hard part. The never faltering willpower part. Caroline was determined to pull it together, to succeed. No way did she ever want to go through this again. *And Jesus, look at that mess in the mirror.*

Knowing her body needed nourishment, she boiled a couple of eggs and made toast. While she choked it down, Caroline also chewed on the fact she had given up for the first time, a previously foreign concept to her. After some thought, she concluded it was a necessary evil to solve the more significant issue: her withdrawal, a reason she could live with, but vowed never to put herself through again.

After cleaning up the kitchen and herself, she went outside in hopes of finding something to do. *I need to keep busy to stay on the recovery train. But all summer? What could this place possibly offer for an entire summer?* Her fragile confidence began to waver.

# Chapter VI

Once outside, looking at the overgrown property and gardens, Caroline remembered Will's suggestion and saw a way to keep herself occupied. *Am I seriously considering tackling this project? I must be going crazier than I thought.* Not seeing any other options, she talked herself into giving it a go. *I do love a challenge.*

Her tenacity restored, Caroline pulled her ponytail through an old baseball cap of Will's and headed for the shed. Knowing the cleanup needed more than what her mom's gardening bench offered, she went straight for her dad's tools. After putting on work gloves and goggles, she grabbed the chainsaw, and within an hour, determined that it ran on gas, how to fill it, and figured out the safety switch. Proud of herself, Caroline cranked it up, ready the get the party started. After almost being knocked on her butt, she gained control of the beast and went to work, stopping only when her arms felt like rubber and sweat ran down her back and face. Giving herself a mental pat on the back, she decided a break was in order.

Grabbing a cold water bottle out of the fridge, Caroline knew her body needed fuel and made a turkey sandwich. Too dirty to eat inside, she took it out to the porch and forced down half a sandwich while surveying her work. As much as she had accomplished, it barely put a dent in the work to be done. *Well, you needed a project; now you've got one. Get off your butt and keep moving,* she told herself. Downing another bottle of water, Caroline got back to business, clearing and stacking what she'd cut. By the time she finished, the sun was sitting low, and her arms and legs were scratched and bleeding. *I look like I've been in a fight with a bloody alley cat,* she thought and put the tools away for the night.

After cleaning up and making herself eat a light dinner, Caroline ventured outside. But sitting on the porch swing, trying to relax, the past reared its ugly head again, and with it came the overwhelming urge to drink. Back inside, she sat in her mom's rocker and was surprised to be able to read a few chapters of *Little Women*. Even more startling was the realization it wasn't restlessness that eventually made her close the book, but the fact that she was too tired to keep her eyes open. "Good night, Mom," she whispered before she got up, the feeling of warmth still engulfing her. Caroline turned the lights out, brushed her teeth, and crawled into bed. She was asleep as soon as her head hit the pillow.

The sound of an outboard motor on the lake drifted through the window, waking her to a new day. Every muscle in her body screamed in protest when she rolled over to check the clock. She hobbled out of bed into the bathroom and stood long enough under steaming water to downgrade the pain to aches and stiffness. Getting back to work for the day was going to take a lot of ibuprofen and Bengay. Remembering the angry cuts and scratches, she mentally added an antibacterial cream to the list.

After forcing down a breakfast she didn't want, Caroline headed to the general store and quickly found everything she wanted. Except for Dan. "Hello! Is anybody here?" Her heart danced the cha-cha as he came around the corner, making her feel like a schoolgirl.

"Sorry, I was unloading a shipment. Did you find everything you need?"

"I have now," Caroline flirted.

Dan's blush set her insides aglow. *There is something about this guy,* she mused. Noticing the items she held, a look of concern crossed his face, and Caroline laughed.

"I'm fine, just out of shape. I started clearing the growth around the cabin yesterday, and my body is in shock."

Dan grinned, showcasing his award-winning dimples. "You didn't strike me as the physical labor type."

"I'm not, but I need something to let off steam and surprisingly find the work rewarding."

"You do seem a lot less wound up than the last time you were here. No offense," he added sheepishly.

"None taken. I know how fiery I can be. It's part of my charm."

"Well, if you need a hand with the heavy lifting, let me know. I'll be glad to help."

"I just might take you up on that."

Caroline winked and headed out the door. *Well, aren't things progressing nicely?* she thought with a smile and decided to wait a few days before making the damsel in distress call.

Back at the cabin, Caroline used her tailormade first aid kit, changed her clothes, and got to work. By lunchtime, she realized she would need Dan for more than just eye candy. The larger overgrown shrubs and roots were way beyond her capabilities. The idea of watching Dan's muscular body in motion took some sting out of having to admit there was something she couldn't conquer on her own. The daydream made her belly quiver. *Guess you're never too old for a crush,* Caroline reflected and got back to work.

The rest of her day followed the same pattern as the previous one, including her evening visit to the porch swing, which unfortunately bore the same results. Unable to control her thoughts and the craving for a drink becoming unbearable, she retreated inside to her mom's rocker. Not in the mood to read, Caroline curled up with an old photo album and started leafing through the pages of her memory.

She smiled at the picture of her mom and dad sitting on the bumper of the old truck, taken on the day her dad brought it home. The bumper fell off immediately after Will snapped the shot, her parents landing on the ground rolling with laughter. Caroline recalled it being the first time she recognized them as a couple in love and not just parents. The polaroid of her and Will standing on the dock holding two fish brought back lazy days spent fishing in the quiet intimacy of a siblings' bond. She couldn't remember a single time her brother had complained about her tagging along. There were pages of pictures with family and friends enjoying a feast at the picnic table or sitting around the campfire. Caroline could almost hear the chatter and laughter, smell the burning pine, and taste the toasted marshmallows. *I guess I had some good times here after all.*

But it was a particular photo of her and Will that touched Caroline's heart the most. Taken on the day she fell out of a tree, it portrayed a banged-up kid sister being read to by a doting older brother. Her mom, having scolded her countless times for climbing trees, was short on sympathy. Any consoling ended once she saw her daughter needed neither cast nor stitches. After she applied Mercurochrome to Caroline's skinned knees and elbows, produced a package of frozen peas for the bump on her head, she had treated her daughter's bruised ego with sternness. "Maybe now you'll learn." Only Will had understood what had motivated her. He'd grinned at his sister's tear-streaked face and shook his head.

"Aren't you gonna ask me why?"

"No. I know why. You did it to prove you could. You realize you could've broken your neck, don't you?"

"I know, but I had to try." Caroline had winced in pain as she put the peas against her head.

“Come and sit, Wonder Woman. I'll read to you and take your mind off the pain."

"I can read to myself. I'm not a little girl anymore."

Will had rolled his eyes and patiently waited her out. Eventually, grumbling all the way, Caroline handed Will a book and curled up beside him.

Will. Her brother understood her and always had her back. Every time. That photo reminded Caroline of their connection, the mutual unconditional love and loyalty. Hit with an overwhelming urge to hear his voice, she called him. Will answered with a sleepy hello.

"Sis, is everything okay?"

"Of course, why wouldn't it be? I just wanted to say hi."

"At two o'clock in the morning?" he groaned.

"I was looking through an old photo album and … "

"Ahhhh, I see. And you started missing your awesome brother. I can understand that."

Caroline heard the humor in his voice and played along. "Let's go with adequate."

"Are you kidding? A lesser man would've thrown in the towel years ago."

"I guess you're right; I've never been easy, have I?"

"Easy no. Worth it, yes."

"Thanks for always being there, Will. I love you."

"Love you too, sis. Hey, does this mean I'm out of the dog-house?"

"Maybe. I'll get back to you on that."

Will chuckled as he hung up, and Caroline was relieved all was well between them again.

With her stomach's earlier knot of anxiety replaced by warm contentment, Caroline went to bed and slept the sleep of a carefree child. Well, almost.

Her new alarm clock, the outboard motor, woke her at six o'clock. Even with so little sleep, Caroline felt rested and raring to go. After a hot shower that she loved and a breakfast she almost enjoyed, it was time to plan. Caroline calculated there were two more days she could handle on her own before Dan was needed for the heavy work. Once he was done, the restoration of her mother's gardens could begin. Caroline was surprised (and more than a little worried she was losing it) to discover how much she was looking forward to it. Shaking her head at the wonder of it all, she cranked up the chainsaw and attacked the workday.

In late afternoon, a black pickup pulled into the yard just as Caroline was finishing up. Dan jumped out and gave an appreciative whistle as he surveyed all she had cleared out.

"I admit, I didn't think you had it in you."

Caroline put her hand on a cocked hip. "I can do anything I set my mind to." *And that includes you, my friend*, she silently added.

Dan raised his hands in defeat. "I stand corrected."

Caroline grinned. "Good to hear. That said, if your offer is still on the table, I could use your help."

"Of course. Lead the way and show me what needs to be done."

After surveying the shrubs, roots, and small stumps that needed to be removed, Dan estimated he would need a full day. "Let me check with Emmy to see when she can cover the store, and I'll let you know. It should be within the next day or two."

Caroline linked her arm through his and leaned in too close as they walked back to the truck.

"That would be great. Are you sure it's no problem?"

Dan gently disengaged his arm, put some space between them, and tugged on the bill of her ball cap. "Nay. Anything for Will's baby sister."

Dan drove off, leaving her with a wave. Caroline was amused by his little maneuver but not the least bit concerned. She always got what she set her sights on, and she was laser-focused on Dan Preace.

# Chapter VII

Caroline woke late the following morning to the sound of rain falling through the trees, explaining why the outboard hadn't roused her earlier. She padded into the kitchen, poured coffee from the automatic maker, draped the afghan around her shoulders, and went out to the porch swing. Tucking her bare feet under her, Caroline wrapped her hands around the warm mug. Comfortably swaddled with the aromatic mixture of coffee and fresh earth filling her senses, she watched the rainfall on the lake, unmindful of the vivid red cardinal who landed on the porch railing. Moments later, when Caroline still hadn't acknowledged its presence, the bird hopped closer and cocked its head in greeting. "Well, hello there," she said and instantly felt her mom around her. *How nice, but odd considering I'm not in the rocker.* Suddenly, she was soothingly lulled into a state of serenity, akin to when her mom held her as a toddler.

Able to sit without thoughts banging around in her head like pinballs, her mind quiet and free of anger, Caroline became acutely aware of her surroundings. She admired a dragonfly sitting on the porch post as if waiting out the rain and vaguely remembered it represented something spiritually. She whispered "bon appetit" to a rabbit eating vegetation under the hammock and mimicked the way his nose wiggled as he chewed. Spotting a regal fox standing in the tree line, head held high, Caroline raised her mug in salute to his beauty. And she laughed at the antics of two chipmunks and a few squirrels scurrying around as if playing hide and seek, oblivious to the weather. Inspired, she stepped off the porch and joined in the fun. Spinning faster and faster, arms flung open, face lifted to the sky, Caroline stuck her tongue out to catch raindrops, fully embracing her inner child. A simultaneous bolt of lightning and crack of thunder sent all creatures, large and small, running for shelter. Caroline giggled with glee and made it onto the porch just as torrential rain swept across the lake. She could have sworn the bird chirped its approval before taking shelter in a nearby pine. *Playing in the rain and making friends with a bird. I really am losing it.* But she had to admit it was cleansing, freeing, and just what she needed.

Chilled to the bone, she stepped out of her wet clothes and sunk into a hot bath. Warm and cozy once more, she toweldried her hair and went in search of a dry blanket. Assuming her mom's hope chest was the best bet, Caroline raised the lid and found more than what she was looking for. Tucked in the folds of knitted and crocheted creations was a journal. On page one, written in her mother's precise and dainty handwriting, were the words *Lakeside Chats with Me, Myself, and I.* She lifted the book from its secret place, gently, as she would a baby bird from an abandoned nest, and sat down on the edge of the bed. *Now, what do I do? Read it? How can I not? Do I even want to know Mom's most private inner thoughts? Can I handle them? Would Mom see it as an invasion of privacy or be willing to share her views with me now that I'm a woman?* Suddenly, Caroline felt her mother's presence for the second time that day and had her answers. She understood, without question, she was guided to the journal and meant to read it.

Caroline lit a fire and took her new find to the rocker. Taking a shaky breath, she opened to the first entry.

*Our fourth summer at the lake, but the first year I'll be staying all season. It would be too chaotic moving back and forth every weekend with the baby. I so love it here, but I'm worried about being alone with the new baby during the week. Bill suggested we hire help, but I refused. I'm perfectly healthy and capable of handling things; I'm just being a Nervous Nelly. Besides, my husband makes good money as a young CPA in the city, but an added expense isn't in the budget right now. Buying a home in the suburbs of Connecticut, even a small one like ours, is expensive. Bill doesn't realize I know this, but I keep track.*

*I've never bought into the silly notion men must shoulder all the financial burden leaving women happily in the dark. Marriage is supposed to be a partnership.*

*I pick up our baby boy and find such comfort. Holding him, soaking in his innocence and love, always instills a feeling in me like no other. I'm in awe of the emotion he ignites within me, the fierce need to protect and nurture. The overwhelming love he inspires in me brings me to a new place deep in my heart. A special place that only mothers possess, I imagine. Bill teases that I'll spoil him rotten, but I instinctively know he is wrong. This beautiful being will never spoil; he is a kind, gentle soul who radiates all things good. No, our Will is exceptional; I know this as well as I know my name.*

---

*Well, it's Sunday night, and Bill left for the city. I sent him on his way with a thermos of coffee and a show of confidence I don't feel. There's no need for both of us to worry. He works hard and deserves these weekends on the lake, and I am determined to do my part to make it happen.*

---

*I can't believe it's Friday already! It was silly of me to be apprehensive. Will thrives in the fresh air, and I feel so refreshed, inside and out. Something about this place is magical. It touches me, calms me. I'm sitting on the porch, watching the critters scurry around nesting, and feeding their young, a reminder I need to start dinner as Bill will be here soon. I still feel like a bride at the thought of being with him, having him nearby. What fun the three of us will have this weekend, our little family. I am one lucky lady!*

---

*The weekend flew by but otherwise did not disappoint. We had long, lazy breakfasts on the porch and made love while Will napped. I threw a conniption when Bill said he wanted to take Will on the boat fishing until he laughed and told me he was only kidding. Still, I wonder. On one of our after-dinner walks, we met Donna and Dan Preace, whose cabin is a couple down from ours. They have a son Dan Jr., the same age as Will, and we all hit it off right away. Donna is coming over Monday, and we're going to try our hand at knitting. I just know we are going to be the best of friends!*

Questions swirled in Caroline's mind: *So, Will and Dan met as infants. Why did Dan only mention camp in high school? And I don't remember the Preaces as part of Mom and Dad's inner circle at the lake. I wonder what happened?*

She threw another log on the fire and continued reading.

*I haven't written in over a month because I've been so busy. Donna and I spend all day together most days, walking in the woods, wading in the water, or sitting on the porch swing, our sons always with us. The two of us talk non-stop and have shared so much in such a short time. We have a lot in common, but there are many differences as well. We agree motherhood is a gift like no other, but we differ on how to raise a child. I believe children need structure and discipline to feel secure and thrive. Donna thinks schedules and rules suffocate free-thinking and crush imaginations. We differ on the role of a wife. I can't imagine not having dinner ready when Bill gets home from work. Donna sees nothing wrong with cereal for supper if she gets distracted during the day. She's the carefree and spontaneous type, while I'm more of a planner and the voice of reason. We are such a good balance for one another, and I can see us picking up some of the other's attributes. How well-rounded we will be! Bill teases that we act like teenagers, always giggling, but I can tell he's happy I've found a friend. I'm sure his mind is more at ease, knowing I'm not lonely all week.*

---

*I instantly took to knitting, but Donna didn't last the first afternoon. She took a short walk instead and returned with wildflowers and greens she weaved into artistic wreaths. True to our characters, my hobby is patterned and methodical, hers imaginative and unconstrained.*

*Today, as we worked on our crafts, Donna nonchalantly asked if I enjoyed sex with Bill. Blushing, I told her, of course, hoping she'd leave it at that, but she pressed further, wanting to know why. I tried to put it all into words but failed miserably. It came out as the usual cliches; tenderness, passion, sharing our bodies and souls, etc. Surprisingly, she didn't laugh at me but asked, "And physically?" My blush turned fire engine red, and I told her the truth. It was a sensation like no other. She commented Bill must be an attentive lover, and my contented smile confirmed it. I teased that her and Dan's sex life must surely be fulfilling with her vivaciousness and free spirit. My friend didn't answer, but her face said it all. When I tried to get her to confide, she just asked me to let it be. How sad someone so full of life is missing out on one of its greatest joys. For now, I will do as she asks.*

---

*Donna was very downcast today, deflated, like a balloon that's lost air. Even more disturbing, she refused to say why. I can't help but think it has something to do with our conversation yesterday. We sat on the porch all day, me knitting and her just staring out over the lake. I finally gave up on engaging her and left her to her thoughts, but I'm so concerned. The only time she seemed aware was to tend to her son. I hope she's better tomorrow. If not, I will drag it out of her. That's what good friends do.*

---

*Donna was still subdued today, so I pestered her until she talked. I was right to think some of it had to do with our conversation. She said, seeing my face so luminous and hearing the passion in my voice as I described how my lovemaking with Bill made me feel, brought back sweet memories of her past. When I suggested she and Dan might get it back once the baby was on a set schedule, my friend gave me the saddest smile, and my heart broke. She wasn't talking about Dan. Donna found their lovemaking adequate at best, but had never felt the passion and emotions I described with Bill in her own lovemaking with Dan. It was a reminder of how much she missed it. My friend confided that sometimes her life feels stagnant and tired. Like she's treading water. Able to keep her head above the waterline but never free to swim. How long can a person do that before they drown, she wonders? Such depressing thoughts and negative observations are so not like the Donna I know. She again asks that I let it be.*

---

*Donna seems more herself as the week goes on, so I assume things are working themselves out. When I told her how worried I'd been, she put her arm through mine, grinned, and joked about how dramatic creative types can be. Maybe. I guess. Still, I'm concerned.*

---

*We have developed a weekend pattern of sorts. Fridays are quiet so that Bill can unwind, and we can catch up. Saturday mornings, the men go fishing while the ladies prepare a potluck for the community get-together. By afternoon, we start to gather for our time. There are horseshoes, bean bag games, croquet, badminton, you name it. The older kids jump off the dock while their younger siblings splash by the shore or play tag. The gaiety and chatter of children, women and men blend to create a harmonized melody—a lyrical song of carefree happiness and friendship. Then we eat, drink, and sit around the fire, building lasting memories for our children and us. Sundays, Bill and I keep to ourselves, enjoying each other's quiet company and our beautiful son. I feel so blessed to have this life.*

---

*I can't believe the summer is over already! We had the last hoorah tonight and said our goodbyes. Donna and Dan were the last to go, and Donna and I cried as we hugged and promised to write. We laughed through our tears, admitting we talked too much for long-distance calls. Oh, how I will miss my new friend!*

Caroline closed the journal, deciding to read one year at a time. She wanted to fully process her mother's thoughts and experiences at the lake and determine how much they contributed to the woman she called Mom. Intrigued but hungry, Caroline put her thoughts away and moseyed to the kitchen to make supper.

# Chapter VIII

Dan called as Caroline was finishing dinner.

"First thing tomorrow morning works for me if it's okay with you."

"Absolutely, what time is first thing?"

"Six-thirty."

"Seriously?"

"Okay, six forty-five," Dan said with a laugh and hung up.

"Is the sun even up at that hour?" she asked the dial tone. *Well, I guess I'll find out.*

Restless, Caroline ventured out to the porch swing. The rain had stopped, and a light mist hung over the lake. A blanket of fog hovered over the trees as if tucking them into bed. With the smell of wet earth and freshly watered pine filling her senses, she pictured her mother sitting in this very spot, writing. It was hard to reconcile the timid young author with the woman

Caroline had called Mom. Her mother was always a confident lady and outspoken when need be. She was an attentive wife but hardly dutiful, as the journal thus far portrayed her. And what happened to the Preaces? They didn't just vanish into thin air. Will and Dan were close in high school. So many questions. Caroline looked forward to following her mother's story, learning how life situations shaped her, helped her grow.

The following day, determined to get Dan to take notice of her, Caroline rose with the sun to get ready. Rugged chic was not a look she had ever created. Her guess was it required makeup to highlight, but not enough to look made-up and hair in a ponytail or braid. *Ballcap or not?* Jeans had to hug the curves but still function. Should she tuck the bottoms into work boots or wear sneakers? Wear the work shirt tied or unbuttoned over a cotton camisole? Decisions made, a final eye to the mirror told her mission accomplished. Caroline gave herself a thumbs-up, amazed the 'hick in the sticks' look took her three times longer to achieve than her corporate power play ensembles. Hoping the effort would pay off, she went to make breakfast.

Sitting on the porch having coffee and toast, Caroline heard the familiar outboard motor approach and saw a small fishing skiff skirt the shore. A man waved as a giant furball splashed into the water and swam ashore. Before she could react, 120 pounds of dog was in front of her, shaking off and soaking her head to toe in hairy lake water. If that wasn't bad enough, the more she yelled, the friendlier the dog became, finally landing its muddy paws on her shirt for a hug and a lick on her face. Laughing, the man whistled, yelled "Charlie," and the dog sat. He tied the skiff to the dock and waded ashore, grinning ear to ear. Caroline let him know by the the look on her face, she was not amused.

"Sorry about that. Charlie loves meeting new friends almost as much as he loves peanut butter. You were a twofer."

Caroline looked down to see the dog finishing her breakfast. "I'll remember to use jelly next time."

"Won't matter; he considers you a friend now. You're a keeper." As if on cue, Charlie leaned on Caroline's leg and nudged her hand for a pet.

"Great. I thought mutts instinctively know when people aren't dog lovers," she said, cringing away.

"They do. Charlie makes it his mission to turn people around. I'm Otis, by the way."

"Caroline," she replied, ignoring his outreached hand. "If you'll excuse me, I need to go change. Mud and Eau de wet dog wasn't the look I was going for."

Before Otis could respond, Charlie bound towards the road, barking and tail wagging. Within seconds, Dan's truck pulled up. "Hey, boy –what a nice surprise!" It appeared Dan was enjoying the frolicking celebration as much as the dog. *Great, so much for well-prepared chic.* While Caroline stewed, Dan and Otis clasped hands and did the half-hug thing guys do.

"Good to see you, my friend! What brings you to this side of the lake?"

"Charlie spotted this lovely lady having breakfast and decided she was worth meeting. But it turns out the feeling isn't mutual."

Dan gave a belly laugh. "Charlie will win her over. He always does." He raised his eyebrows at Caroline as if to scold her to be nice, and she stuck her tongue out at him.

Noticing the equipment hitched to Dan's truck, Otis offered to help. Dan assured him he had it covered but looked forward to seeing him later at the weekly poker game. Ready to take his leave, Otis shook Dan's hand and tipped his hat to a scowling Caroline while Charlie gave a farewell bark. Chuckling on his way back to the skiff, Otis patted Charlie's head. "You've got your work cut out with that one, boy. She's a handful." Charlie just grinned, tongue hanging out, and trotted along, his tail in motion. "I know you like her but can't for the life of me figure out why. She's a bit uppity for my taste."

Caroline watched them walk away in disgust. "Look at what that damn dog did to me," she complained.

"There's no such thing as a damn dog, and you should show Addisen's mayor some respect."

"Otis is the mayor? Well then, he should teach his mutt some manners."

"Charlie's the mayor, and he's done the best he can with Otis's manners."

Caroline rolled her eyes. "Just when I think this place can't get any more backwoods."

"We choose to think of it as quaint. Now, come down off your high horse so we can get to work."

The two of them worked well together. Dan used the backhoe to excavate then drop the shrubs to Caroline, who dismantled them with the chainsaw. Side by side, the pair bundled and tied the debris to load into Dan's truck. At one point, Dan flashed Caroline the timeout signal. "Whoa, slow down a little. No need to push yourself so hard." *Oh, but there so is! If you only knew...*Caroline was fighting down an unexpected burst of withdrawal anxiety. *Christ, will this ever bloody end?* By noontime, she was feeling better, and Dan was happy to be ahead of schedule. Breaking for lunch, Caroline decided to dig into Dan's story.

"So, why, Addisen? You realize there's a great big world out there, right?"

"I know. I've seen most of it and like it better here." Dan laughed at her look of surprise. "Can't believe I'm a world traveler, huh?"

"No, it's not that. I can't believe anyone, after seeing the world, would settle here."

"Well, I have, and I did."

"You didn't answer my question as to why."

"Are you always this nosy?" Dan asked in between bites.

"Only when my interest is piqued. And I prefer the term curious."

Dan smiled, "Okay, I'll give you the Cliff's Notes version. I grew up outside of Washington, DC. My dad was a government contractor, my mom, an amateur artist. They started summering here when I was an infant, their cabin a few plots down from this one. Mom and I would spend the summers, and Dad would chopper in for weekends." He answered Caroline's puzzled look with, "No, not wealthy — connected. Once Mom… well, when it became just Dad and me, he sold the cabin and bought one across the lake."

"I thought those cabins were mostly weekend fishermen and hunters," she said.

"They are, but a few of us are year-round," Dan said. "Anyhow, that's where I met Otis. He and his father were full-time residents, so I stayed with them on summer weekdays while Dad worked. Otis and I are like brothers."

"Where was Otis's mom?"

"She died of a brain aneurysm a week after he was born. His dad, broken-hearted, never remarried."

Caroline, dying to know what happened to Dan's mom, prodded,"It must be challenging to grow up without a mom."

All she got for her effort was a shoulder shrug as Dan stared off in the distance. "You make do I guess."

He continued his story. "I lived life in the DC fast lane, got a degree at Georgetown in international business, became a globe trotter, and was successful at what I did. Being a hot shot was fun for a time, but it got old for me. And I only felt whole, grounded when I was here. So, when old man Cavanaugh said he was retiring, I saw my way. I bought his store, moved into the cabin, and never looked back."

"Any regrets?"

"Only one. The time we're wasting yakking instead of working." Dan's dimples appeared as he headed towards the backhoe. "Let's get back to it, Princess."

*Fine, have it your way, for now,* she silently told him. *But know that I always get my man.*

The sun was almost down by the time they finished, and Dan was late for his poker game. After a quick goodbye, Caroline dragged herself into the cabin, too tired to survey the fruits of their labor. A shower did nothing to revive her, so a bowl of cereal was supper, and she went off to an early bed. Her plan was to revisit all she'd learn from Dan, but sleep was not willing to wait. Within seconds, Caroline was snoring softly while visions of tequila danced in her head.

# Chapter IX

Excited to start planning her gardens, Caroline was in the kitchen early when the outboard sounded through the morning air. Hearing Charlie's belly flop and seeing him gallop towards the cabin, she quickly hid between the open door and wall. When his bark and happy dance drew no response, Charlie resorted to whining and scratched at the screen door. Otis came ashore to call him back.

"Come on, fella, we're not welcomed today. Maybe tomorrow." Dejected, the dog lumbered off the porch, looking back in hopes his master was wrong.

"You do know he can smell you behind that door, right? If you're determined to avoid him, you'll have to get more creative than that." Otis waved goodbye to the screen door, and they headed back to the skiff.

*God damn him, now I feel guilty,* Caroline seethed. *And over a dog's feelings? I've chewed people up and spit them out without blinking an eye for Chrissake.* Many times she had undermined coworkers to win over their accounts, or got underlings fired for not doing her bidding. *What is happening to me?*

Shaking it off, Caroline took her mug outside and started to visually create her gardens. Unfortunately, all her mind registered was empty dirt spaces and a sense of dismay. "What the hell was I thinking?" she asked the cardinal sitting on the porch railing. "I have no clue what to do with this mess." A thought instantly popped into her head. She'd go to the store and buy a book on gardening. Most likely, there was one in the cabin, but she wanted to see Dan. "Thanks for the idea, friend." The bird cocked its head as if to say "you're welcome" and flew off. *"Great. Now I'm conversing with a bird."* She shook her head, grabbed the moped and headed for town.

Happy to find Dan behind the counter, she thanked him again for his excavating help, then asked about gardening books. "Sorry, I don't carry any." He thought for a moment, then snapped his fingers. "But I do have a plan that would be way more helpful. Why don't you come over for dinner tomorrow night, and we can discuss it?"

*Now we're talking,* Caroline thought, cocked her hip to the side, and with her best come hither voice, cooed she'd love to. After getting the time and cabin number, she all but skipped out of the store. It felt good to know she still had it. Until a confidence-sapping thought smacked her in the head. She hadn't had sober sex since Jack. What if she sucked? What if she hated it?

What if… At this point, Caroline gave herself a talking to. *Snap out of it out of girl! I'm sure it's like getting back on a bike. You might be a little shaky at first, but you'll find your balance and hit your stride. God knows you've had enough practice.* Feeling better, she hummed a tune all the way home. After all, she had never sucked at anything, least of all sex.

The thought that Dan had meant just dinner never occurred to her.

With her entire day now free, Caroline grabbed her mom's journal and headed for the hammock. She hoped year two would answer some of her questions. She had so many questions…

*It feels so good to be back! Will is walking now, and it's next to impossible to keep him from the water. I don't mind. I could sit and watch him splash around all day. And he loves to dig in the dirt while I weed the gardens. Today he dug up a worm and was so gentle with it. We put it down, and he watched intently as it burrowed into the soil. He even clapped his little hands when it finished the job. How I love seeing the world through his eyes, everything a wonder, a joy, a lesson. Yet another blessing my sweet boy gives me.*

*The Preaces arrive this weekend, and I can't wait to see Donna. I miss her infectious laugh and devil-may-care attitude, not to mention our talks. Letters are lovely but no substitute for the real thing. I do hope the boys still get along.*

---

*We kicked off the season Saturday with the first get-together. I love how we all fare from different states, cultures, and backgrounds but come together as a community in Addisen every year. Donna and I didn't stop talking for a minute, and I doubt we will all summer. It was like no time had passed. And the boys were inseparable; I was silly to have worried.*

---

*Bill left for the city this morning, and I miss him already. I couldn't sleep last night from sheer happiness. I laid awake in my husband's arms, replaying the day over and over in my head, like a favorite movie. Watching Bill feed Will breakfast while reading him the Sunday paper. "Never too young to be informed," he said when I pointed out he was only fifteen months old. Watching the two of them in the lake, Bill tirelessly keeping Will afloat on his tummy, racing him through the water, pretending to be a speedboat. Father and son, napping in the lounge chair, Will on his father's chest, his little hand resting on Daddy's face. I loved when Bill grabbed me in the kitchen, gave me a passionate kiss, and our son giggled and clapped. Bill announced, "That my boy, is how to kiss a woman good and proper." My husband saw me blush, touched my cheek, and whispered, "Still my beautiful bride." After supper, we lit a fire, and Bill read "Cinderella" aloud while I rocked our son to sleep. He carried Will to bed, then held me close, and we danced around the kitchen as if it was our first dance at our wedding. After we made love in front of the fire, still cloaked in our lover's glow, my Price Charming thanked me. For loving him, giving him my heart, a beautiful son, and the life of his dreams. Imagine that? Him grateful for me, the luckiest lady alive. Just when I think it's impossible to love him more, I do.*

---

*Donna and Dan came for the afternoon. What a difference a year makes. There's no time for knitting, wreath making, and chatting with two toddlers to chase around. Thank goodness for their afternoon nap. While the boys slept, we caught up. I confided my little secret to her, even though it was too early to tell Bill. We jumped around and squealed in celebration, both hoping it would be a girl. Sharing the news made it seem more real. Again, I marvel at how connected we are, even though we are opposites. Maybe it's because we awaken a little piece of each other's inner self: that small part people tap down to appease their whole. Hmmm... food for thought. Whatever it is, I cherish our bond.*

---

*I am devastated I lost the baby. I feel numb, broken, inadequate. Thank goodness for Donna.*

*She consoles me and cares for Will, allowing me time to mourn. Her friendship offers me someone with whom to grieve, someone to understand. She holds me until my tears run dry, and I drift into sleep to escape. She listened without judgment as I sobbed my anger at God, then prayed with me while I asked His forgiveness.*

---

*As we sat on the porch swing this afternoon, a red bird landed on the railing. Donna told me the bird was the spirit of my baby girl, telling me she'll always be with me. She whispered cardinals are visits from loved ones on the other side. I found such comfort in that. I believe now my heart can begin to heal. What would I do without my friend?*

---

*The weekend is coming, and I must pull myself together for Bill. He didn't know the joyous news, so why have him suffer the crushing loss? I am determined to save him from heartbreak. My daughter's spirit perches nearby, head cocked, watching me write, and I smile at her. I swear she winks before flying away. I'm confident she'll be back, and with that knowledge comes serenity. Maybe not peace exactly, but less pain. Donna comes out and leans on the very spot the bird vacated and cocks her head. It makes me laugh. After I explain what's so funny, she throws her head back, and looking to the sky, laments how she wishes she could fly. My beautiful, whimsical friend. Donna points to my lap, and I see a dragonfly seated on the journal. She explains they represent change, transformation, inner strength. Its presence means I'm evolving, growing into my own, becoming more assertive. I certainly don't feel strong, yet she says I am; she envies my strength, my confidence.*

*Donna envies ME? I am baffled by this. Uncomfortable, I suggest we wake the boys from their naps for lunch. She just smiles and agrees.*

The rest of the year's entries were uneventful, only the easy flow of life at the lake. Caroline closed the journal and started to review what she'd learned.

As a child growing up, Caroline had a sense of her parents' love but never gave it much thought. Reading about them as a young, playful couple, full of passion and affection, was heart-warming. She now knew and appreciated that their devotion to one another provided the prominent foundation on which they'd built a family. She looked forward to learning more about their love as it matured and grew.

Donna Preace. Clearly, the two women had a unique and profound relationship. The influence they had on one other, the intuition they shared, the connection. They trusted each other enough to open their minds to the other's views and ways. Adopting some, not understanding others, but always willing to listen and accept. When Donna shared the spiritual meaning of cardinals and dragonflies, her mom embraced it, and it eased her pain. It was not a belief a practical woman like her mother would have readily adopted. Yet, she trusted her friend enough to believe.

Her mother lost a baby and never told a soul other than Donna. That spoke volumes about the depth of their bond. What happened to their friendship? Where was Donna now? Intuitively, Caroline knew not to press Dan. Maybe, hopefully, year three would shed some light on it.

Caroline remembered her own recent encounters with a dragonfly and cardinal. Was she about to go through a transformation, a colossal change? Was the cardinal her mom's spirit?

Tired of trying to put the puzzle together without all the pieces, Caroline decided to go for a swim. She figured it was about time one of her bathing suits got wet. *Let's just hope it doesn't fall apart*, she thought on the way in to change.

# Chapter X

Caroline spent the following day with excitement dancing in the pit of her stomach, like a schoolgirl on prom day. Humming Carley Simon's song "Anticipation" she contemplated which strategy to use on Dan that evening. Cool and aloof? A playful tease? Eager and ready? Shy and innocent? She snorted at the last idea. She was years past innocence. She decided to trust her intuition and play it by ear. Now, what to bring? Usually, it was a bottle of red and a bottle of white, but that was out, as was dessert. The last time Caroline remembered baking, it was in an Easy Bake Oven. *I might have to go empty-handed.*

Needing to pass the day and too antsy to sit and read, she grabbed some gardening tools and started to prep the gardens. As she worked, Caroline daydreamed of the night ahead. Dan's naked body pressed against hers, limbs intertwined, their scents mingling as they made love. Lost in that delicious thought, she didn't notice the outboard motor had taken the day off.

In the early afternoon, Caroline decided to take a walk to kill time. The lovely wildflowers brought Donna to mind and inspired her to collect flowers and green. Her arms full, she headed home and was joined by a butterfly. "Well, hi there, you gorgeous creature. Thanks for the company. I now know you represent change and transformation, growth and renewal. Between you and my dragonfly friend, I guess I'm in for an awakening. Just please, don't make it a rude one; I'm more fragile than I look right now." The butterfly briefly touched down on her shoulder before flying away.

Back at the cabin, Caroline arranged the flowers in a vase then began to get ready. Following a long, hot bubble bath, she applied a scented lotion that always drove her lovers crazy, painted her toenails, and did what she could with her roughed-up hands. Going for soft and sensual, she left her long curly hair down and chose a flowing sundress that showed just the right amount of cleavage. Deciding to forgo a slip allowed a hint of the curves shrouded beneath the semi-sheer fabric. A long pendant nestled provocatively between her breasts was the final touch. "Nicely done," she said to the mirror and gave her reflection a sexy wink. Full of confidence and tingling with anticipation, Caroline headed out the door and stopped dead on the porch. How was she going to get there? Dressed as she was, riding the moped was out, and it was too far to walk in the dark. Just as panic was setting in, Caroline heard the dreaded outboard approaching.

"Noooo," she screamed. "Keep that wet mop away from me!" Otis chuckled as he docked the boat.

"Charlie's home. I figured you wouldn't be receptive to his enthusiastic hello this evening. Though I have to tell you, his heart is broken, being left behind and all."

"He'll live. Why are you here?"

"Nice to see you too. Dan asked me to come and get you. He didn't want you riding the moped in the dark."

"He's a gentleman, for sure."

"Yeah, a real prince. Need a hand coming aboard?" As much as Caroline wanted to say no, she knew better. Before she could hold out her hand, Otis grabbed her by the waist and pulled her into the skiff, holding her a second too long. Caroline wiggled free and plopped down, precariously rocking the boat. Otis roared with laughter as she let out a terrified yet furious scream. "Can we get this over with as soon as possible?"

"As you wish, milady. Nice finery, by the way." Otis pushed the outboard full-throttle, lifting the nose of the skiff out of the water. With Caroline clinging to the sides for dear life, they crossed the lake in record time. Safely docked on the other side, Caroline found her voice and let him have it.

"Have you lost your fucking mind?! Are you trying to kill me?"

Otis gave a low bow. "You requested as soon as possible, milady. I am here but to serve you."

Caroline looked down at the windblown mess that was her dress and knew her hair had to have fared far worse. "Did anyone ever tell you you're an asshole?"

"Daily. What time should I pick you up?"

"I have no intention of going home tonight."

An odd expression passed over Otis' face before he broke into a slow grin. "I see. I look forward to hearing how that works out for you." He tipped his hat and pointed the skiff toward home.

*What an infuriating jerk of a man,* she seethed. Taking a couple of deep breaths to calm down, Caroline smoothed her hair as much as possible and headed towards her fantasy evening. Barely able to tap down her enthusiasm, she rang the doorbell, and hearing footsteps approach, put a seductive smile on her face and prepared to plant a soft, teasing kiss on Dan's lips.

"Hi, I'm Dan's wife, Emmy, and you must be Caroline. He's told me so much about you, I feel like I already know you. Please, come in! Dan got held up at the store, but he should be home soon."

Stunned, Caroline had yet to cross the threshold. *His wife?!* Noticing her guest's look of shock, Emmy, concerned, guided her through the door.

"I see Otis must've treated you to his speed ferry ride. He can be a real pill sometimes. Can I get you a glass of water?"

Caroline managed to shake her head no and asked for the bathroom. "Down the hall and to your left." Emmy said.

Numb, she made it down the hallway and used the privacy of the bathroom to regroup. A wife. Emmy was his wife, not a part-time clerk as she had assumed. How had she missed the signs? Were there any? What a scumbag Dan turned out to be. Or maybe not. Had he led her on, or had she led herself on? Either way, there was no time to work through it all now. She would wait to play shrink at home. Right now, she needed to straighten up, suck it up, and get through the evening. Caroline splashed water on her face, arranged a smile, and headed back down the hallway.

Dan arrived soon after, planting a kiss on the wrong lips and giving a longing look to the wrong woman. Hiding her disappointment, Caroline made small talk and helped set the table. Over dinner, she learned Emmy was Dan's solution to her gardening woes. "Emmy has an eye for design and knows horticulture inside and out," he said with pride.

"Dan gives me too much credit. There is always more to learn, but I'm getting there. I would love to open a business someday."

"Then why don't you?" Caroline asked.

Emmy kissed Dan's cheek and started to clear the table. "Money," Dan answered for her.

Over dessert, Emmy offered to stop by in the morning to give Caroline ideas and different options. Not her original Preace of choice to work with, but she needed help. And as much as she wanted to dislike Emmy, Caroline found herself drawn to her as the evening wore on. Maybe it was her aura of quiet strength and calm. Or her girl next door looks and friendliness. Whatever she had, it certainly appealed to Dan. It was obvious he was as taken with her as she was with him. Getting more depressed by the hour and feeling her head start to throb, Caroline thanked them for a lovely evening, and Emmy offered to drive her home. They pulled into her driveway and another perfunctory thank you, a "see you tomorrow," and, at last, Caroline could let her face fall.

Emotionally spent, she curled up on the bed, fully clothed, and let her guard down. Her mind wasted no time in taking over. Too tired to think, but with so much to sort through, Caroline knew sleep would not come without alcohol. Defeated, she got undressed, swallowed some aspirin, and got a cold cloth for her eyes. Back in bed, she got comfortable and let her mind have at it.

After seeing Dan and Emmy together, it was clear their love was the real deal. No way Dan was a player. That meant Caroline had totally misread the situation between her and him. Objectively reviewing their encounters, she had to admit they were innocent enough. She did all the flirting and just assumed he was responding. Her charm never failed, right? But this was sober. When was the last time she worked her magic straight? Being honest with herself, it was the last time she wanted more than a one-night stand. It was with Jack. She groaned at the thought of his name and decided to leave that tangled mess for another day. At any rate, it seemed without tequila as her wingman, she couldn't trust her instincts concerning men. And that scared the hell out of her.

Her mind moved on to the next thought. Addisen was a place of real people. Honest, friendly, open, ready to lend a hand. A close-knit community. She had automatically assumed Dan's eagerness to help was due to an attraction to her. Accustomed to the city's indifferent and counterfeit people, she didn't recognize genuine when she saw it – much less know what to do with it. What registered most was how little of the former and much of the latter defined her. Caroline had always loved the city life, thrived in its fast pace, chrome-plated, impersonal environment. It was where she belonged. Or was it? That life was growing more distant by the day. But surely she didn't belong here. Feeling untethered in limbo, Caroline drifted off to sleep, craving a drink. Again.

# Chapter XI

Emmy arrived in the morning, her smile as inviting as the plate of homemade blueberry muffins she held. "I thought they'd go nicely with coffee while we discuss your options. But first, I need to look at the areas you want to plant." Caroline led the way while Emmy measured and noted the location of each plot. Armed with the info, she sat at the picnic table to sketch while Caroline warmed the muffins. Once they settled in, Emmy started by suggesting they reshaped the garden along the cabin's front to add contour and then extend it around the wooded side and back. She recommended ornamental grasses at the corners and a rose vine to climb along the porch front for the lakeside. As far as the two stand-alone plots, Emmy thought one would make an excellent little bird sanctuary, with a birdbath, house, and feeder nestled among wildflowers and maybe a shrub or two. In her opinion, she would eliminate the other – overkill. Caroline looked at her in amazement. "You came up with all this in the time it took to make coffee?"

Emmy shrugged. "I just get a vision and roll with it. Time to hear your ideas."

"I don't have a one, and if I did, it couldn't top this. I love it all, especially the little bird resort."

They each buttered a muffin and began to plan. The nursery, an hour away, would take all day, so they decided to go the next morning. Emmy would help Caroline choose hardy and low-maintenance plantings, and she and Dan would tend to things in the offseason. *Like I'll ever be back*, Caroline thought.

"You'll return – trust me. Addisen gets in your blood and travels straight to your heart."

"What, you read minds too?"

Emmy grinned. "You don't exactly have a poker face, my friend." She then suggested they spend the rest of the day edging the new borders.

They hadn't worked long before a barking cloud of dust came down the road. With Otis' pickup still rolling, Charlie jumped out and hurled himself into Emmy's waiting arms. After lots of whining and giggling, slobbery kisses, and "good boys," the dog approached Caroline, sat regally with his nose in the air, and offered his paw. Caroline tentatively shook it and begrudgingly tapped his head. Feeling knighted, Charlie pranced away with his tail held high. Emmy and Otis lost it.

"What in the world was that?" Emmy asked in between peals of laughter.

"Charlie's formal greeting, I guess," Otis snorted. "Never seen him that well-mannered before."

Happy to see two of his favorite humans amused, Charlie joined the party, racing around them in circles. Caroline felt a pang of loneliness watching the three friends, so connected and carefree. She couldn't remember the last time she shared such a moment with anyone. Once the festivities ended, Emmy headed to the bathroom, and Caroline braced herself for the inevitable onslaught. Otis didn't disappoint.

"I see you made it home last night after all."

Caroline pounced on him like a wildcat, green eyes ablaze, disgust dripping from her every word. "You should've told me! Did you enjoy your little juvenile prank? I bet you giggled all the way home like the naughty boy you are." She was livid. "A real man would never set up a lady that way."

No longer amused, Otis moved within a breath of her. "You had already set yourself up, milady. And I'm not inclined to help someone who had just called me an asshole." Hearing Emmy come out the screen door, he took a step back and replaced his sneer with a forced smile. "And what, exactly, would you know about real men or ladies?"

Before Caroline could unleash more fury on him, Emmy returned, ending the conversation, if not the tension. She sweetly asked Otis to help by digging the side and back gardens and waited until he was out of earshot. "Glad I arrived in time to stop the skirmish from escalating into a bloodbath," she said.

Caroline responded with silence. Emmy shrugged and watched as Caroline continued to slam the edger into the soil with enough force to bore through rock. "Yep, Otis owes me one for sure. I have a feeling that could've been his head."

The three of them worked through the afternoon with Charlie lending his expertise in digging, and by dinner time, the gardens were ready to plant. Surveying their work, Emmy suggested lining the borders around the front with rocks for a nice rustic touch. But that was for another day. They decided on the morning's departure time, and Emmy lingered, making small talk. With the static between Caroline and Otis still strong enough to stand everyone's arm hair on end, Caroline didn't blame her for not wanting to leave them alone.

Once Otis made his exit, Emmy turned a penetrating gaze on Caroline. "So. What's up between you and my cousin?"

"Great. Perfect. The most obnoxious, tactless man I know is my only friend in Hicksville's cousin."

"I know him. And I've seen the way he looks at you when he thinks no one is watching. Trust me, he's attracted to you and fighting it."

"Attracted to me? He goes out of his way to be sarcastic and insulting to me."

"It seems to me that flies both ways. A protective shield, for the two of you, maybe?" Emmy shared one more observation as she got into her truck. "My gut tells me the tension between you two isn't all anger."

After Emmy left, Caroline collapsed in the hammock and allowed the breeze to cool her hot skin and bring her boiling blood to a simmer. Slowly the birds' songs replaced the banging of anger's pots and pans in her head, and the smell of pine was like a balm for her frayed nerves. Feeling calmer, Caroline started to unwind the tangled ball of her psychological libido.

She knew there was something to what Emmy said. Part of her roiled with rage around Otis, and another fought not to let that rage turn into lust. She had a fierce, visceral need to take him. And to be ravished by him. Not like lovers, but animals; a fight to the finish. A competition to see who came out on top. Caroline smiled at her pun. That was her attraction to him, she decided. The challenge to beat him and his uncanny ability to get under her skin and stay there. To win.

Not that he wasn't good-looking if you liked the type. A little short for Caroline's taste, he wore blondish curls in a ponytail, and his brown, almost black eyes, missed nothing. A ready grin sat in the middle of a nicely groomed beard, and an air of nonchalant confidence rounded out the look. Sexy, yes, but not what drew her to him.

Then there was Dan. A short time ago, she was preening like a starstruck teenager, preparing to lay herself at the altar of infatuation. That's all it was, considering it took a nano-second to get over it. Her grief was more self-pity than love loss.

Dan had followed a year of random, drunken sex – threesomes that consisted of her, Don Julio, and faceless guys to punish herself for losing Jack. Or was it self-preservation? Maybe a bit of both, but harmful nonetheless.

Jack. Caroline's perfect mate. Handsome, debonair, brilliant, and successful, he was the most sought-after bachelor in Manhattan. Caroline had found his raw ambition and determination to accomplish his end goal, politics, incredibly sexy. She fell head over heels when he supported and encouraged the same traits in her while she clawed her way to the top of advertising. Where most men found her overbearing and too focused, Jack celebrated her fierceness. He understood it and respected her for it. Until he didn't.

When they met, he was working on connections, his sights set on running for District Attorney down the road. Their first couple of years were total bliss, living hand in hand. They were connected at their center, finishing each other's thoughts and sentences. The couple looked forward to their lazy Sundays in bed, spent alternating between making love and strategizing, finding both equally erotic. Weeks were long, with late nights at work and accompanying one another to networking events. They became known as a must-invite power couple, Caroline basking in the envious glances single socialites sent her way. And then Jack announced his run for District Attorney. Sundays in bed became speeches at brunches. He no longer had time to escort her to events but became furious when Caroline was unavailable for his.

Whenever she sought his counsel on a problem or situation, Jack would stare at her impatiently or take a call in the middle of their conversation, his attention never to return. Yet, he expected her to be accessible, no matter the cost. Their connection became one of resentment, then downgraded to silence. When Caroline tried to approach him about the issues, Jack exploded, accusing her of pettiness and jealousy because his career was moving faster than hers. He felt Caroline was deliberately forgoing public appearances with him as payback for his inability to accompany her to events. He called her self-centered for continuing to put the demands of her career before his needs. Gutted by his words, she allowed anger to wrap protectively around her and threw him out.

A month later, Jack was seen with a new ornament on his arm, smiling up adoringly at her shining star, and Caroline was left wondering if he was right. Was she too self-centered to be loved? Maybe. But one thing she knew for sure; she would never again give another man her entire inner self. She wouldn't survive another betrayal of her authentic, naked being.

Her ego bruised and swearing off love, she resorted to meaningless, drunken sex for a year, followed by an immature, ill-thought-out infatuation, and now fought a craving for angry, competitive sex. *Christ, I'm a shrink's wet dream,* she concluded.

With that thought in mind, the first mosquito took a bite, forcing her inside before others showed up to draw their drop of blood.

The metaphor was not lost on her.

# Chapter XII

Caroline waited for Emmy on the porch swing, surprised at how eager she was to get going. She was also annoyed by the pang of disappointment she felt at not hearing the outboard. Seeing Emmy's truck approach, she threw the peanut butter toast she'd made for Charlie in the bushes, telling herself it was the dog she missed.

Caroline hopped into the truck, and Emmy's sunny warmth immediately embraced her."Do you ever have a gray day?" she asked.

"Not many, and certainly not today. I'm off to do what I love with a new friend I enjoy. What's better than that?"

Caroline shook her head and buckled up. "How do you do it? What's your secret to managing your internal weather?"

"It's just my makeup, I guess. Why frown when you can turn it upside down?"

Caroline made a gagging noise and rolled her eyes, earning a giggle from Emmy.

"I knew that would get you."

"Seriously, Emmy, tell me what allows you to be so confidently optimistic."

The two women rode in compatible silence while Emmy collected her thoughts. Eventually, she said, “I mean, really, it all comes back to one thing: Dan. He’s the reason why I have this faith in favorable outcomes; that all things good and true will prevail.” Emmy shared her story.

She had no memory of life without Dan. They were only four when his father bought the cabin next door to her uncle's. Summer meant long, unpredictable hours for Otis' dad so Emmy’s mom, his sister, moved in to run the household. A few years older, Otis preferred shadowing his dad to playing, leaving Dan and Emmy on their own. Inseparable from the start, they shared an unbreakable bond, an uncanny oneness. Each summer, they would meld together as if no time had passed and would feel each other's presence even when apart.

As they got older, they exchanged countless letters, sharing their innermost thoughts and fears. Their “first time” together flowed naturally and unplanned as if meant to be, like all other aspects of their connection had occurred. No matter the distance or circumstance, they were always each other's safety net. The one constant in life to count on.

"And it's still that way today," she said.

"Wow. Lifelong love from childhood is practically unheard of for our generation," Caroline said. An incredulous thought hit her. "Wait – are you saying the two of you have never had sex with anyone else? Ever?"

"I never said that. How do you think I came to appreciate what Dan and I share? Being in love doesn't end a young girl's curiosity. There was a brief encounter with a fellow camp counselor during the summer of my junior year. And a semester-long affair with a professor my sophomore year of college."

"Extracurricular activities with a professor? I'm impressed!"

Emmy tried to appear unflustered, but her red cheeks gave her away.

"What about Dan? Any known dalliances on his part?" Caroline immediately felt the playfulness slip from her friend.

With a nervous sideways glance, Emmy said, "That's not my story to tell. Let's talk about you. What makes you tick? Makes you so…"

"Hard?" Caroline offered.

Emmy smiled. "I was thinking more like crusty."

Caroline started to tell her about Jack when Emmy stopped her. "Wait, you were an adult before falling for someone?"

"Yeah. I mean, I dated a lot, shared my 'first time' with Tommy what's-his-name in high school, and had my fun in college, but nothing serious. I saw relationships as needy and time-consuming and never found anyone I cared about more than my goal. I was always determined, even as a child, but it became a drive to be the best at something big once I got to college. I decided on advertising at the largest firm in the city and stayed laser-focused to the top. It was just my personal priority, I guess."

"Hmmm... Okay. Let's hear about this Jack."

Caroline shared the Jack saga for the first time, including the emotions it provoked in her throughout the relationship. She was surprised at how easily she'd opened up to Emmy.

Wiping her tears, she continued, "So, lesson learned. I'm incapable of putting a man ahead of my goals even when I'm crazy in love. Like Jack said, self-centered to the core."

Emmy pulled off the road and turned to stare at her friend, anger burning in her eyes. "That's bullshit. Jack switched the dynamics of the relationship from equal support to all about him. And when you didn't, couldn't accommodate him, he belittled your career, called your commitment inadequate, and attacked your self-confidence. Jack's the self-serving narcissist here, not you. The only thing you're guilty of is putting your trust in a jerk."

Conceding Emmy may have a point, Caroline promised to mull it over when she got home.

"No maybe about it. Geez, Caroline, for someone so smart and successful, you sure are clueless about men."

Considering her recent, private insights, Caroline knew Emmy was right on target.

As they turned into the nursery, Caroline's enthusiasm started to match her friend's. They stepped out of the truck and into a sea of life. Various blossoms' colors, so vibrant in the sun, blended yet stood apart like a brilliant kaleidoscope. She felt high as the perfume created by their mingling scents filled her head. Everything moved as one in the gentle breeze, the unified pulse of nature's beauty. Caroline was awestruck. Seeing her friend was overwhelmed, Emmy suggested she lay out a base model to give them a place to start. Then they could tweak each garden to suit Caroline's taste. With a plan in place, the two were soon knee-deep in perennials, bushes, and ideas.

Hours later, waiting for the truck and trailer to be loaded, Caroline reflected on their accomplishment. She hadn't worked that well with anyone since playing sports as a kid. And even then, there was the underlying competitiveness to be the best. She felt no threat from nor need to one-up Emmy, only compatibility and easiness. Impulsively, she hugged her friend.

"What's that for?"

"Just for being you."

"Looks like your crust is starting to flake."Emmy said with a smile.

"Maybe it is." Caroline wasn't quite sure how she felt about that.

The ride home mirrored their good mood. They sang along with the radio and kept the conversation light. When the truck pulled up to the cabin, they were treated to Charlie's unexpected but enthusiastic welcome home. Otis looked up from positioning rocks on the final border and gave a low whistle as he eyed the loaded truck.

"Did you ladies buy out the entire nursery?"

Both women were too busy admiring his day's work to answer. He had placed rocks of different shapes, colors, and sizes to border the front gardens and the birds' resort.

Caroline stared in appreciation. "It looks like the gardens are wearing handmade necklaces. They're beautiful."

"Working with rocks and stones is a hobby of his," Emmy explained. "And Cuz', you've outdone yourself this time! Glad you picked up on my not-so-subtle hint yesterday."

While unloading and placing plants near their designated garden, they noticed the new loam. Emmy smiled. "Talking to Dan last night, I mentioned concern about the quality of the soil. It looks like he also took the hint."

Emmy quickly departed to fix a thank-you supper for Dan when they finished, and Caroline offered Otis a drink before he left. Drinking iced tea on the tailgate of his truck, parked by a lake, a dog at her feet felt like a country song, laid back and comfortable. Then he opened his sarcastic mouth.

"I'm enjoying the 'thank-you' beverage."

"You're welcome."

"By the way, it's good to know you now look forward to our morning visits. Charlie enjoyed the breakfast you left him in the bushes. And for future reference, I like my coffee black."

Infuriated, Caroline jumped down off the tailgate and turned to him. "Why do you always have to goad me?"

Otis was silent a moment, appearing to mull something over. Eventually, he said, "Because you're haughty at times, milady. I consider it a public service."

Caroline took the glass of iced tea from his hand and slowly dumped it on the ground. "Uh oh, looks like it's time for us to go, Charlie." Otis closed the tailgate and sauntered to the driver's side door, Caroline's glare hot enough to burn holes in his back as she watched him pull away. *If I ever serve that man coffee, it will be laced with arsenic,* she vowed.

# Chapter XIII

Caroline's phone woke her at midnight. Her heart raced when she saw who was calling. "Hector? Is Will okay?"

"Hello to you, too, sunshine. Of course, he is. Why wouldn't he be? This call is work-related."

"You called me in the middle of the night about PG&G? Have you lost your mind?"

Hector snorted, "Since when is midnight the middle of your night?"

"Hector, I'm in no mood to banter with you. What is so imperative you had to wake me?"

"Wake you? The Caroline I know would just be getting started."

“I'm hanging up."

"Okay, okay. Just having some fun. I'm calling to give you a head's up. Maci’s on fire. You need to start taking her calls."

"No, I don't."

"Caroline, you know your clients better than anyone, and PG&G needs your input."

"Exactly. If I share that knowledge, there's no reason to keep me. It's called an insurance policy." She said.

"Okay, Just letting you know the landscape."

"Speaking of landscape..."

Caroline, her excitement audible, filled him in on her project. There was silence when she finished.

"Are you still there?"

"Ah, yeah, I'm delighted for you, but I have a question. Who are you, and what have you done with our Caroline?"

"That's a question I've been asking myself a lot lately."

They said their goodbyes, and too wound up to sleep, Caroline reached for the journal on her nightstand.

*Our first community get-together is tonight, and I'm anxious to see Donna face to face. Her letters this winter lacked their usual creative insights and cheery tone. I sense a shift in my friend and intuit she needs me. Together we can set anything right.*

---

*The Preaces never showed last night. Worried, I walked to their cabin this morning. Donna answered the door, and I was struck by her eyes straight away. Eyes that had always twinkled with such life held confusion and fear. Instead of promise, I saw haunted defeat. Seeing me, she sobbed, and I held her, rocking her like a baby until she had cried herself dry. I was relieved to see Dan healthy but saddened to see him unaffected by his mother's upset – as if it was a common occurrence. Seeing no sign of Dan Sr., I gently urged her to come home with me. Bill could entertain the boys while we talked. Once at the cabin, I could see a wave of relief wash over her leaving exhaustion on her mind's shore. I suggested she lay down for a while, and, grateful, she agreed. Soothed by the calmness of feeling safe, she slept the day through.*

*I put the boys to bed and tried to knit, but my hands trembled with emotion. What on earth is going on within my friend's world?*

---

*The boys were up early, not wanting to waste a single moment of a brand-new day. I took them outside so as not to disturb Donna, but she joined us within the hour. Cloaked in a fog, a blanket across her lap, she sat watching her son, silent tears rolling down her cheeks. What seemed like an eternity later, she reached for my hand and laid her head on my shoulder. I begged her to talk to me, assured her whatever it was, we could fix it together.*

*She brought my hand to her cheek, calling me her sweet, innocent Meri, then whispered some things are too broken to repair. Poppycock was my response. Every situation holds a solution, and in everything, there is hope. She smiled faintly and teased me for saying poppycock. Just talk to me, I pleaded! And she did.*

*Donna had fallen in love her freshman year of college. Head over heels, can't eat, obsessed kind of love. It was mutual. She never thought these kinds of emotions, awakenings, pure joy could exist between two people. Even all these years later, I could hear the wonder of it all in her voice. When I asked Donna what happened to him, she went still. I felt the turmoil of emotion churning inside her and saw it etch pain, indecision, and fear on her face. I assured my friend I was there for her, no matter what had happened. She finally spoke. "Her. It was a her."*

*Stunned, I tried not to react, which, of course, is a reaction in and of itself. Things like this didn't happen in my buttoned-up college world. I babbled something about people experimenting with all sorts of things in college, trying to find themselves. Donna gave me a sad smile and said that's what they'd told one another at graduation. They ventured out into the so-called real world and had no contact for years; until their college reunion last September. The reconnection was powerful and instant as if no time had passed. It was a tornado of intense desire and love denied that swept them away, rendering them helpless in its funnel. The ensuing affair was inevitable. Living a double life was taking its toll on Donna. She knew the relationship had to end but didn't possess the strength of will needed to do it. She took both my hands in hers, stared into my eyes, and quietly stated, "I'm a lesbian, Meri. My life, as you know it, is a lie."*

*For one nanosecond, a minute tick in time, I tensed to stone and fought the urge to recoil. But my perceptive friend felt it and pulled her hand away. I explained it was the initial shock of hearing it, nothing more, but the damage was done. I watched her faith in my loyalty and trust in our friendship escape from her pores and evaporate into thin air.*

*Donna stood, made some excuse about dinner, and took Dan home. I went inside, and it was my turn to cry.*

*Holy crap, I didn't see that coming,* Caroline mused. With any chance of sleep now gone, she took a sip of water and braced herself for the year's remaining entries.

*Donna and I continue to get together for the boys, but things are not the same. I apologized profusely, and she graciously accepted, but it's all pretense. I'm trying to come to terms with her admission, and she's feeling deserted by the only friend she trusted. It's a bloody mess, but I'm determined to somehow heal the wounds.*

---

*Donna called and canceled lunch today. Dan Sr. was sending the chopper to pick her and Dan up. She wasn't sure when or if they would return. She hung up before I finished asking if everything was okay.*

---

*It's only been a few weeks since Donna left, but the worry makes it feel like forever. Thankfully, Bill called, and he's taking a few days off. He'll be here tomorrow morning. A dose of family togetherness is just what I need.*

---

*As soon as I saw Bill's face, I knew something was wrong. I was right. Donna is dead. Suicide. My heart stopped, and I felt my life's blood drain from my body. I swear, for an instant, I died too. Bill held me while I fell apart, then gently tried to patch the pieces back together. To my repeated question of why he handed me an envelope addressed to me. "Dan found this in her things. Maybe it holds the answer."*

*I tentatively opened the envelope as if I were dismantling a bomb. I chose to read it on the porch swing, where Donna and I had shared so much of ourselves. There, on tear-stained paper, were the last words my friend would ever share with me.*

Caroline lifted the yellowed paper from between the pages and carefully unfolded the letter.

*My Dearest Meri,*

*I fear I'm about to disappoint you for a second time, but I see no other way.*

*Lila's husband (that's her name, Lila. Isn't it beautiful? So lyrical to say) suspected she was having an affair and listened in on one of our phone calls. Appalled, he contacted Dan, who demanded I bring his son home immediately. His son. My mother-in-law was there, grabbed Danny from my arms, and ran out the door. I haven't seen him since. Dan promises I never will. Oh Meri, the ugly, vile things he said to me. The disgust in his eyes, the venom in his voice. He gave me an hour to collect my belongings and get out.*

*I have begged him to let me see Danny. I try to tell him I'm the same loving, adoring mother I've always been, and a boy needs his mother. But he's too angry to hear. He sees me as a monster, a freak. His mother caught me standing across the street yesterday, trying to catch a glimpse of my baby. Dan was furious. He said he was getting a restraining order against me. Me. Danny's mommy. The person who loves him more than life itself.*

*So, you see, Meri, all the love has been drained from my world. Without love, there is no color or magic. No beauty or hope. No reason to live. No Danny. I could never be happy with Lila knowing it cost me my son. But selfishly, how can I lose her again? How can I live with the thought my baby will grow up thinking I loved someone more than him? How can I bear to know the shame and stigma I have caused my son to shoulder? I can't. None of it is possible. I have caused enough pain. It is best for everyone if I'm gone. Don't you find it ironic and cruel that being in love is the very reason I've lost all that I love?*

*My constant grief, pain, and guilt suck all the energy from me. What have I done to my son? My family? Lila's family? It's too painful to breathe. I must stop. I will sit in a warm bath and drain the color from my body to match the gray of my world.*

*Please don't mourn me, my friend, I'm going to a kinder place, and I promise to visit you from time to time. I will be the faithful, most brilliant red cardinal to perch on your porch.*

*Donna*

Caroline refolded the letter, tucked it safely back in its resting place, and read the final entry of the year.

*Bill sat down next to me and put a protective arm around my shoulders. Dry-eyed, I handed him the letter to read. When he finished, I railed against Dan, trying to blame anyone but Donna for her death. He told me Dan was devastated, guilt-ridden. His hurt and anger over the affair were so intense he refused to see his actions cut Donna to the*

*bone. His intention was never to keep her from Danny forever but to punish her. I scoffed. It was easy for him to say now. My husband gently suggested I put myself in Dan's shoes. Maybe someday I will, but I need to be angry at someone, and he's it for now. And me. I am livid at myself. Would Donna have called had things been right between us? Could I have saved her? I will never know. But I do know this: I swear on my best friend's soul, no one I love will ever doubt my loyalty and support again, no matter the circumstance. Never.*

Feeling her mother's heartbreak through her words, Caroline instinctively hugged the journal to her chest to ease some of her mom's despair. With a heavy heart, she drifted off to sleep.

# Chapter XIV

Still feeling melancholy and with little sleep, Caroline was relieved when Emmy called to cancel. Dan needed her to cover at the store, and Otis had unexpected business. They agreed to start planting early the next day and said their good-byes. She took a cup of tea out to the swing and turned her thoughts to the journal.

Clearly, the friendship with Donna had a profound effect on her mother, as did her death. Donna's bohemian mindset opened her mom's world to the wonder of nature's art, as well as spiritualism and self-care. Her friend's carefree attitude guided her mom away from the restraints of a supposed proper lady, opening a world where both could co-exist. Unfortunate for her, she also learned – the hard way – the hurt an ill-conceived judg-ment could inflict, no matter how brief or unintended. In Don-na's death, her mother grasped the importance of unconditional acceptance and unwavering support of those you love. All lessons she applied throughout the remainder of her life.

Caroline now knew the Meredith McMerritt who raised her, and Will was a product of her upbringing and Donna's influence. The sensible, no-nonsense, “roll-up your sleeves and get it done” attitude was a family trait. The open-minded playful visionary was born of an unlikely yet undeniable bond between two women. The combined influences resulted in an admirable, affectionate woman, confident in who she was and what was right – right being whatever it was for the individual, what fits for them. Her mother believed there was no one universal way to live. If you were kind and fair, you deserved respect. That belief was why she accepted Will's gayness and Caroline's sometimes self-destructive behavior without fail. Not that she didn't voice her opinion or offer her unsolicited advice, but out of concern. Never in judgment. They grew up knowing even if Mom didn't fully understand, she was always in their corner. A gift to her children born of a tragic loss.

Caroline grieved for Donna Preace. She couldn't fathom the volume of pain and confusion that flowed through her veins. An agony so debilitating, only death would stop her misery.

If born later, Donna would've found the world a more inclusive place, one that celebrates people's differences. She and Lila could have lived openly without fear of losing Donna's son. But it was a time before gay relationships were accepted, or even spoken of in most circles. Hence her mother's knee-jerk reaction.

Donna's son. Did Dan know how and why his mother died? If so, how was he able to come to terms with it? Will might know. Dan said they were close friends at camp. Caroline dialed her brother's number.

"Good morning. How's my favorite brother?"

"Uh oh, you must want something."

"You know me so well."

"That I do. What's up?"

"I need information. Talk to me about Dan Preace."

Silence.

"He said you were close when you counseled at summer camp together."

Silence.

"Hello?"

Will let out a long sigh. "What do you want to know and why?"

Caroline gave him a synopsis of their mom's journal, Donna's letter, and her developing friendship with Emmy. She was concerned, and yes, curious if Dan knew the truth. Also, she didn't want to bring up anything Emmy didn't already know. After a lengthy pause, Will took a deep breath and dove into the murky waters of the past.

Yes, he and Dan were buddies. One night, the last summer of high school, Will had invited Dan home for dinner. Apprehensive, not knowing how much Dan's father had told him, their mom shared only casual tidbits of her friendship with Donna.

Will remembered he and Dan found it odd that no one had ever told them their parents knew one another, much less were friends.

"Dan left, and Mom confided to me how close she and Donna had really been. How it touched her heart to see so much of Donna in Dan. And that the best of her friend lived on in her son. Teary-eyed, Mom handed me a letter. It was Donna's suicide note. If Dan wasn't already aware, she was afraid his father would have to tell him now, knowing he had met her and Dad. She wanted me to be prepared, both for him and me. She had seen immediately that I had a major crush on him, something I thought I was hiding so well.

"She patted me on the knee and gently said, 'He will need a friend, Will, only a friend. Be one for him.'

"I was scheduled for an overnight at camp and headed back to work. Once I did a headcount and announced lights out, I went to douse the campfire. I found Dan, dazed and alone. Seeing me, he let go an empty sob. I sat him down and waited until he was ready to share. Mom had nailed it. Dan knew nothing. He'd believed his mom died in an accident when he was three. To this day, I've never seen someone so churned up inside, so broken.

"He kept asking questions I couldn't answer. How could his mom willingly leave him? Didn't she love him? Her baby? And his father, lying all those years. Why? Because she was gay? So fucking what. His father's bruised ego meant more to him than telling his son the truth? Knowing I was in over my head, I stayed quiet and just listened. Dan's emotions ran him in circles until he was physically drained and too dizzy mentally to think. Far too angry to go home to his father, I suggested he sleep at camp, then come home with me in the morning. I knew Mom would know what to do.

"I woke in the middle of the night to Dan getting into my bunk, and I put my arms around him while he cried himself to sleep. Understand, I was a seventeen-year-old boy with raging hormones in bed with my first crush. In his present state, I knew Dan would be vulnerable and open to any form of comfort. But I also knew he wasn't gay. Any move on my part would've been selfish and damaging to him. So, remembering Mom's words to be a friend, a seventeen-year-old kid made a man's decision. I grew up some that night, albeit it was not easy.

"In the morning, I took Dan home to Mom. She took him in her arms, and for the next two weeks, they were inseparable."

"Wait, I don't remember him staying with us."

"That was the year you announced how unfair it was you couldn't stay overnight at camp, just because we owned a boring house across the lake. In the name of peace, Mom and Dad bought you two weeks of overnight."

"Oh yeah, I remember. I was quite obnoxious about it."

"That's an understatement."

Will got back to the story. Working her magic, their mom told Dan endless stories of his mother, painting the picture of a free spirit, her heart invariably open, warm, and inviting to all. She portrayed Donna's mystical connection with nature and spiritualism and helped Dan capture it, as Donna had done with her. They took endless walks together, as she and Donna had, their mom showing Dan the world through his mother's creative eye and imagination. Most importantly, their mother shared how Dan's mom adored him, how her world revolved around him. He wanted every detail of the relationship between mother and son that she'd witnessed, and she lovingly shared it all.

"Once confident Dan could handle it, Mom gently approached Donna's frame of mind at the time of her death," Will said. "She confessed she was also baffled how her friend could do such a thing, something so violent and complex to process for those left behind. But after her grief, and yes, some anger, subsided, she'd tried to see things from her friend's perspective. The stigma placed on gays at the time was devastating, and the child custody laws were against them. Mom was convinced that Donna did what she did to save Dan from the pain her choices would inflict on his life. She also retold Donna and Lila's college love story to give Dan a sense of what his mother stood to lose again. Only this time, she would also lose her son.

"And finally, she shared awareness, a point of view, that time and healing had allowed. 'Your mother had no way of knowing how drastically times would change,' she told him,. 'I believe she ended her life out of hopelessness. She loved you too much to lose you to prejudice or expose you to unfair judgment and couldn't bear the thought of you being out there and her not able to be with you. She wasn't thinking clearly, if at all, but I believe, in her heart, she felt she was doing the best thing for you.'"

"Did Mom show him the letter?"

"No. Mom didn't want to inflame Dan's anger towards his father. Instead, she suggested his dad had kept things from him to shield him from hurt. Mom nudged him towards the idea both his parents intended to protect him, no matter how misguided. And it worked. Dan decided to go home and talk things through with his dad."

"And that was it?"

"Pretty much. I don't know if Dan stayed in contact with Mom after we left for college, but I never heard from him again."

"We hit the jackpot in the parents' department, didn't we?"

"That we did. Now let me get back to work."

Caroline hung up, shaking her head. For a Podunk town in the backwoods of Maine, Addisen certainly had some stories to tell.

# Chapter XV

The following day dawned with drizzle and fog. *I guess there's no planting today,* was Caroline's first thought. She heard scrapping outside the cabin, threw on her sweats, and went to investigate which critter was visiting so early in the morning. She found Otis digging holes aided by a mud-caked Charlie.

"Good morning, milady. Sorry if we woke you. Something's come up, and I can't make it later. I wanted to get the biggest shrubs in the ground for you and Emmy."

"You do know it's raining?"

"A warm drizzle is perfect for planting. It makes the transfer from pot to ground less traumatic for the plants."

Caroline resisted the urge to reach over and wipe a smear of mud from his face. Uneasy with the tender thought and afraid it showed on her face, she quickly covered it with a snarky laugh.

"What's so funny?"

"You're quite the sight – as wet and covered in mud as Charlie. You look like a little boy who's eating mud pies."

Otis self-consciously wiped the mud off his face and bit back, “So, that’s your choice of sleepwear? Sexy. Must drive all the men crazy.” He smirked at her old sweats and thread-worn T-shirt.

Caroline drew herself up a little taller. "I sleep nude," she said provocatively, outlining her figure with her hands. "Picture that if you dare."

Otis slowly gave her the once over. "I do, multiple times a day."

"Pervert."

"Tease."

"I'm going to have a cup of coffee."

"Remember, I like mine black."

Caroline kissed her middle finger, waved it at him, and headed back inside, wondering how two adults could act so childishly.

Emmy and her perpetual sunny attitude arrived around eight o'clock, carrying an extra rain slicker and boots for her friend. "This is awesome! Mother Nature is giving the gardens a head start with this weather. We should thank her." Caroline suited up, mentioning she would've preferred staying dry and letting the hose take care of watering later.

It wasn't long, though, before she found herself enjoying the elements. It brought back early childhood memories of playing in the rain with Will. That feeling of pure happiness and abandonment. A carefree time of enjoying the moment, despite any negativity thrown in their way. Carpe Diem, as the saying goes. In her teen years and adulthood, she spent her life not only dashing out of the rain but through her days, with no time for lighthearted merriment or nostalgia. *Yet one more thing I need to work on,* she thought.

Thanks to Otis's earlier work, the gardens were finished by mid-afternoon. Caroline learned Dan was on an overnight trip and suggested Emmy stay for an early dinner. While her friend got cleaned up, Caroline rummaged through the fridge and found precious little. When Emmy shuffled out of the bedroom in her borrowed sweats she found an embarrassed hostess who informed her cereal was on the menu. Emmy told her no worries and waved a hand towards the bathroom. A tantalizing aroma filled the cabin as Caroline washed up, making her stomach growl. She entered the kitchen and found Emmy at the stove, adding sautéed peppers, onion, and garlic to a skillet of sauce.

"Where did you get all this?"

"Right here. I found onion, pepper, eggs in the fridge, garlic, beef bouillon, rice in the cupboard, chicken breast, and a bag of frozen peas in the freezer. A little imagination, some soy sauce, and voila! Fried rice of sorts. I hope you don't mind."

"Mind? It smells amazing! Once again, I'm in awe of your creative instincts." *Much like Donna's,* Caroline thought.

Caroline lit a fire, and they took their bowls into the sitting area. "It's times like this I'd love a glass of wine."

"I'm afraid those days are gone forever, my friend," Emmy said.

Caroline looked at her in disbelief. "How did you know about my, um, problem?"

"Because I had the same issue years ago. I know the signs."

"Do tell."

And Emmy did.

After college graduation, she relocated to DC to move in with Dan. She knew his life in DC was different than the lake but wasn't prepared for the side of him she'd never seen. How at home he was amid the sophistication, glamour, and pretense. He was comfortable, at ease, while she felt like a fish out of water. It was the first and only time Emmy had felt a disconnect with him, and it threw her completely off balance. But she knew Dan was the one and determined they have a life together, tried to adjust. She soon learned a shot or two before a dreaded cocktail party took the edge off. A couple of drinks and too much wine got her through tedious hours-long dinners. The liquid confidence also helped her hold her own when Barbie Doll women threw themselves at Dan. Emmy hated her job, hated the city, and hated their life there. Worse yet, she felt utterly inadequate and phony. Things came to a head when Dan started traveling overseas for business and was gone much of the time. She started drinking at home to curb the loneliness and to stifle her building resentment towards Dan.

On the day she woke up fully clothed next to an empty bottle of vodka, mad at the world and hating herself, Emmy had to face the trouble she was in. She showed up on Otis' doorstep with nothing but the clothes on her back and a resolve to climb out of the hole she had dug. She called Dan and explained what he already knew; she could never be happy in DC. Crying, they said what Emmy feared was their final goodbye. After a year spent in Europe, Dan came to his senses and home to Addisen, buying the store and a ring.

"So that's what he meant when he said he only felt whole here." Caroline shared the conversation she'd had with Dan.

"Was that chat before or after you set your sights on my man's jeans?"

The look on Caroline's face sent Emmy into a fit of giggles. Caroline began to stutter an explanation when Emmy hushed her.

"I figured you didn't know he was married as soon as I opened the door. That provocative stance and sensual look were definitely not meant for me. I thought you were going to plant one on me before you realized I wasn't Dan."

With tears of laughter streaming down her face, Caroline asked why she hadn't said anything that night.

"Why would I make you feel worse than you already did? Besides, I know he's as clueless as he is irresistible. I assumed he didn't see the signs, so hadn't mentioned a wife."

"You were right."

Caroline cleaned up the kitchen, and the two friends settled back in with a cup of tea. After a quiet moment, Caroline wondered out loud, "So, we drank. We know your reason; what's mine?"

Emmy answered without hesitation. "Because you felt less than. As if you'd failed somehow. And you were unhappy with your life and who you'd become."

Caroline shook her head no. "I mean, I felt less than when I failed with Jack, but my life was fast-tracked and still where I wanted to be. I chose to sleep around because it was emotionally safer, easier, and less time-consuming than a relationship. No. I was in the right skin for me."

"Really? Sure you weren't ready to shed that skin and didn't allow yourself time to contemplate it? Maybe the ending of Jack exposed a softer Caroline you weren't ready for, so you drank to avoid meeting her. And to steer clear of any introspection."

Caroline gave a nervous laugh and shook her head no. "I've always been sure of who I am and brutally honest with myself about it. I'm driven, ambitious and tough as nails; I don't know any other way."

"My point exactly. Perhaps there is a shift occurring within that you need to explore. It's just an observation."

Emmy spotted the journal on the side table and asked what Caroline was reading. Hearing it was a diary of her mom's time at the lake, Emmy became pensive. Testing the waters, Caroline asked if she knew of the close friendship between her mom and Emmy's mother-in-law.

"Yes, of course. Dan credits your mom for saving him at a critical time. Sharing her insight and stories of his mother helped him gain perspective about her death and his father's lies. It was a great comfort to him. He would retell the anecdotes to me, and I'd watch as the script your mom had presented him became a full-featured film in his mind. She gave Dan his mom."

Caroline wiped a tear away. "Mom was a special lady."

“You're speaking in the past tense. What happened?"

"An icy road and a tree. I try to find some solace that death was instant, and my parents went together, but the pain and loss are still raw all these years later. Being an orphan is indescribable at any age." Caroline had never said that out loud to anyone, even Will, and was struck by how easily she confided it to Emmy.

After a respectable silence, Emmy asked if the journal held any reference to Will and Dan's relationship. Caroline told her no, but she had asked her brother about it, and Emmy caught her breath. "So, you know."

"I know they were good friends, that Will had a massive crush on Dan, but knew he wasn't gay, so never acted on it."

Emmy shook her head. "I'm sorry, Caroline, but that's not true. I saw them at camp, sleeping together, curled in each other's arms like lovers."

Confident her brother would never lie to her, Caroline set her straight. "You saw them the night Dan learned the truth about his mother. He was too upset to go home, so Will took him to the counselors' cabin. Dan climbed into my brother's bunk crying during the night, and Will held him to comfort him to sleep. Nothing happened, Emmy. My brother told me it took all the willpower he had not to take advantage of Dan's vulnerability, but he didn't. He knew that wasn't what his friend was looking for or needed."

"All this time, I was convinced they had a fling that summer! Dan was so confused about everything, and I thought he was acting out, experimenting. It turns out I was more confused than he." Emmy sat shaking her head in disbelief.

"So that's what you meant by not your story to tell."

Emmy nodded. "I didn't know when, or even if, you knew Will was gay. Plus, I never told Dan what I saw or suspected. It was so many years ago it seemed best to leave it in the past."

Caroline was struck by Emmy's devotion to Dan and her respect for Will's privacy and told her as much. Emmy shrugged it off. "It's just the right way to be for me."

"Well, it's admirable, Emmy, and you should be proud. That degree of character is rare." *Unheard of in some circles,* she silently added.

# Chapter XVI

Caroline threw another log on the fire while Emmy talked about her upbringing. Raised in western Massachusetts, hers was the quintessential small-town childhood. She was the only child of two doting parents, both teachers, who were civic-minded and involved in charities. They passed their core values on to their daughter by example, and though strict, were always fair. Emmy was a cheerleader, homecoming queen, prom queen, and voted class president all through high school. The only downside? Dan didn't live in town.

"Wait – so you didn't date all through high school?"

"Of course I did, but only casually. Dan already held my heart." Ignoring Caroline's eye roll, she continued. "I got a scholarship to college, graduated with a liberal arts degree, and the rest you already know."

After Caroline shared her beginnings, the two women contemplated how they had developed into their present selves. Both raised by parents with similar values in a loving environment accounted for their parallels: their sense of self and loyalty, fierce protection for those they love, and passion for a purpose. Yet, they also had contrasting personality traits and had chosen a much different path. Emmy's nature was calm, forgiving, nurturing, easy-going, and Caroline's was driven, aggressive, demanding, afire. Emmy projected an air of serenity, and Caroline a gale wind of restlessness. Emmy lived a quiet life in rural Maine; Caroline had a fast-paced existence in NYC. Why the drastic difference when their origins were so alike? They reflected quietly for a time until Emmy broke the silence.

"I think we are all born with a certain temperament that's pre-ordained," she said.

"Interesting concept," Caroline replied. "Determined by what? God? Genes? An abstract entity? A previous life? All the above?"

"I've never delved that deep into the philosophy of it, but it would be a great conversation to have some time."

Caroline yawned. "Agreed. A time when we haven't planted all day, and you don't need to open the store at the crack of dawn."

Looking at the clock, Emmy concurred and left her cozy spot to head for the door. With a warm hug, and a promise to call soon, Emmy was on her way. Locking up for the night, Caroline realized she had nothing to do tomorrow. No plans or purpose. An empty day. The very thought of it sent her mind reeling. With a shaky sigh, she got ready for bed, hoping for a good night's sleep. Fearful of what awaited her in the morning, she was grateful for her physical exhaustion and the fact there was no booze around. She wasn't sure she could've fought the beast off at that moment.

Sleep managed to dissipate her fear, and Caroline woke determined to tackle the task of, well, doing nothing. Coffee in hand, she headed for the porch swing, now a welcoming space and no longer one to avoid. She tried to remember the last time her day was a blank slate. Even as a child, it seemed there was always a plan. Caroline was most apprehensive about spending time in the company of only herself, no longer sure who that woman was or if she even liked her. She had always been secure in her role as a cutthroat career diva, but this hiatus had her second-guessing herself. Was Emmy right, and the Jack situation had given her a glimpse of a softer side? Was that the reason for the self-destructive path of the past year; to keep her buried? Did Caroline fear she was missing a step and used alcohol and sex to cope? Or had the rat race become less appealing, requiring an outlet to stay driven? Was it a little of everything? Or none of the above; simply a temporary character glitch? And what on earth was happening here in Addisen? Just outside of two months, tea had replaced tequila and fresh air cigarettes. Gardening had overtaken landing a new client as her passion, and friendship her balm instead of mindless sex. She was even growing fond of a dog for Chrissake. Caroline knew permanently living this life would never be enough, but could she go back to her win at all cost lifestyle now? Just as her head was about to explode, a cardinal landed on the railing, and Caroline remembered (heard?) her mom saying, "Baby steps, sweetie."

"You're right, Mom. There's no need to conquer all on day one. How do I stop myself, though? What can I do to make my mind rest and take things one step at a time?"

In answer, the bird flew to the empty birdbath and cocked its head, making Caroline laugh. "Water. Got it." She filled the birdbath, then moved on to the gardens around the cabin. Caught up in the tender, albeit foreign, feeling of nurturing, she complimented the different blossoms as she watered and promised to do her best to help them thrive. Enjoying the warmth of bonding with nature, Caroline's mind cleared, and her heart lightened. She rounded the lakeside corner of the cabin and found the cardinal perched on the swing, waiting. "Thanks for the distraction; it was just what I needed," she said. As if satisfied, the bird flew off, and Caroline went to retrieve the journal. She had begun to see the role her mother's diary played in leading her to introspection and transformation, its influence causing her to look deeper within. The written words and experiences provided Caroline her mother's guidance even in her absence. It was a gift she knew would help her sort through the chaos as well. Sitting in a beach chair at the water's edge, Caroline put her feet in the water and opened the diary.

*Another year. After Donna's death last season, I went back to the city early. It was too challenging to be here with my grief so raw. I'm glad I did. It allowed me time to sort through my anger and sorrow without soiling the memories of our friendship in this beautiful place. Bill learned Dan sold the cabin, and I am relieved and saddened at the same time. I couldn't imagine watching Dan and Will discover new adventures together without Donna. Yet her son is all I have left of her. Will is too young to remember his buddy year to year, but Donna and I dreamed of them being lifelong friends. Wouldn't a true friend stay in Dan's life for his mother's sake? Would his father allow it? What if Dan remarries? So many questions to examine.*

---

*Bill left for the city this morning, and I summoned the courage to sit on the porch swing without my friend. Watching Will play with his trucks, loneliness washed over me, and I began to cry. All the questions that have haunted me return. Was I selfish? Will should have his friend, and I needed to be one for Donna. I had no doubt she would watch over Will if I were gone. But how? I know they live in DC, but without the lake, when would I see Dan? He's too young for letters and calls. Dan sold his cabin without a word and left no contact information. Was it an oversight made in grief or a need to sever ties with painful memories?*

*With my head about to spin out of control, a brilliant red cardinal landed nearby. I smiled through my tears and said hello. The bird hopped from bush to bush as if to entertain and distract me from my thoughts. It inspired me, made me want to move about and have fun too. I called for Will, and we took a walk around the yard, exploring. At three, he has endless questions about everything. He wants to know why trees are tall and flowers are not? Why rocks are in our yard, and who put them there? Why do bees sting and birds fly? What makes sand? His mind absorbs my pared-down answers like a sponge soaks up water.*

*We spotted a butterfly flitting through the garden, and I shared his excitement. More questions. How do butterflies eat? Where are their mommies and daddies? Do they sleep? Out of answers, I suggested we take an ice cream break. We sat on the porch with our snacks, and the cardinal joined us. I silently thank my friend for redirecting my day from gloom to light and reminding me of the importance of balance. I can't solve everything at once. Will broke into my thoughts, telling me to hurry and finish my ice cream so we could explore some more. I shook my head no. "Baby steps, sweetie. One thing at a time." The cardinal chirped and flew away.*

---

*Saturday night. Fearing questions about the Preaces, I told Bill I wasn't looking forward to the get-together. We decided the best response to be, "They asked us to keep their confidence, and out of friendship, we agreed." It worked, and we only had to repeat it a few times before the word spread. Once that was out of the way, I enjoyed seeing everyone and catching up. I found it soothing, like a salve for an open wound. Being here is good for me. The continuity of traditions coupled with the tranquility of nature is bound to heal me fully.*

---

*I've been so busy it's been a month since I visited these pages. I'm grateful for the cardinal's advice that first day. Whenever negative thoughts threaten to take over, I frolic instead. Will and I splash in the lake, walk through the woods, and find shapes in the clouds. He helps me collect wildflowers and pine to make wreaths like Donna used to do. Mine aren't nearly as lovely, but they remind me of the life and beauty that once lived inside my friend. I find when I immerse myself in the tranquility and peace here, the happier memories surface. More and more, thoughts of Donna leave me with a smile instead of tears.*

*Fully appreciating nature is one of the many gifts Donna gave me. Gently, it has provided answers to my questions. I am not selfish; I'm respecting Dan's surviving parent's wishes. I need to trust in his father's love to do what is best for him. I am confident it's the right way to go.*

---

*It's dawn on our last Saturday of the season, and I haven't slept a wink. I sit here on the swing, trying to summon the courage to tell Bill we're having a baby. I'm afraid to say it out loud, to make it real. I don't think I could bear another miscarriage. As I write, the cardinal lands on the railing, and an instant calm comes over me. Suddenly, I'm confident this baby will be alright. And it's a girl. I am positive it's a girl. I now have no doubt the bird is Donna, caring for me from the other side. I whisper thank you and go in to wake my husband with the news of our blessing. My healing is complete.*

Caroline closed the journal, grateful for her own cardinal. “Thanks, Mom," she whispered.

# Chapter XVII

After reading her mom's latest entries, Caroline chose to follow in her footsteps and set about achieving mindfulness with Mother Nature's help. Having always lived life on the move, being present only in the moment wasn't going to be easily achieved. She decided to approach it as her new project. In typical Caroline fashion, she attacked the task head-on and all in. It only took a few days for her to realize mindfulness was not accomplished in a New York minute; before she understood, the mind, like any instrument, can only be mastered with practice.

To help on her quest, Caroline took long walks in the woods. The forest provided a cocoon-like sanctuary, allowing solace and solitude. She was grateful the pine needles carpeted her footsteps, allowing the life around her to continue uninvaded. She listened for the sound of twigs snapping as deer roamed looking for food and noticed how the thistle would shake as bunnies scurried about their day. Caroline loved hearing the squirrels chatter as they chased each other in play and the sound of woodpeckers high in the trees. She equated the birds beckoning one another in their different songs to her mom calling her and Will in for dinner. Sometimes Caroline pictured herself as a woodland fairy to experience the walk from a different perspective. A tiny being in a gigantic environment, still able to appreciate the beauty and magic even with the threat of danger. *A mentality I'll strive for in my world,* Caroline decided. Inspired by her mother's writings of Donna, she found herself collecting nature's gifts. Berries, pinecones, boughs, various wildflowers, even abandoned bird nests. *Yet another pathway opened to me through your words, Mom.*

The following week Emmy stopped by to check on the gardens and spotted Caroline's treasures on the picnic table. "What's all this?"

"Sometimes I'm drawn to things on my walk, and I feel the need to bring them home."

"You could create some nice-looking wreaths with it."

"No, you could. I wouldn't know where to start."

"Baloney. Different colors and textures appeal to you, so now it's just a matter of learning how to assemble them. Besides, you're in advertising; art is already in you."

"Visual art, my friend, not crafts."

"A minor detail," Emmy said with a dismissive wave.

She offered to provide the needed supplies and a lesson, Caroline promised a nice lunch, and they agreed on Saturday. After Emmy was on her way, Caroline took a quick swim and decided to dry off in the hammock. She was anxious to start the following year's entries, knowing it was her debut into the saga.

*It's the baby's first summer at the lake. Caroline is only three months old, but I swear the fresh air and quiet have calmed her. My daughter rarely sleeps, too afraid she'll miss something, I suppose. Dawn usually finds her and me on the porch swing in hopes of giving Will a few more hours of rest. On the mornings I am exhausted, Donna joins us, gleefully hopping about the railing in celebration. The baby follows the bird with her eyes, stops fussing, and the tension leaves my body. Caroline falls asleep, and I blow my friend a kiss as she flies away.*

---

*As he did when Will was born, Bill suggests a summer nanny. Even though I desperately need help, and we can afford one now, I say no. I'm uncomfortable with someone sharing our cabin and family day and night. Undeterred, Bill finds a workable plan. He posted a notice on the general store's bulletin board for a day nanny. Within two days, we had our pick of high school students eager to make money. We chose twins, a brother, and a sister. Chris would spend Monday and*

*Wednesday with Will and Bonnie Tuesday and Thursday with Caroline. It's perfect; I can have quality time with each of my babies, enjoying the wonders of motherhood. There is no better husband than the one I've got!*

---

*So much for our careful planning. Will prefers Bonnie's company, and Chris has quite the way with Caroline. Not only can he get her to nap, but she also coos more often than cries. I shudder to think what the summer would be without them. I now know I was more stressed and exhausted than I initially thought, which undoubtedly affected my children. Funny, we don't see how atilt we've become until we're upright once again. Is it change that causes us to lean, or do we tilt because a change is needed? Or a little of both? I suppose it depends on the circumstance. I so miss Donna and me mulling over these things together.*

Caroline started thinking about her life. She was beyond tilted at this point; whirling and twirling was a more accurate description. But applying her mother's observation, she gained some clarity as to why. It wasn't losing Jack that put her off-kilter, but his disloyalty. She fully trusted him to accept her as she was and always have her back. Instead, he turned the tables, making his selfishness hers. Blindsided by his gaslighting, she was unprepared for the mutiny. Jack's betrayal of trust, which she previously only awarded to Will, was the reason for her year-long dissent. Instead of tediously working through the knots of her emotions, Caroline chose to hide in her hardened shell, a place where she felt most secure. Or so she'd believed. *Obviously, it wasn't too comfy if I had to be drunk and mindlessly pleasured to stay there.*

That awakening led her to the next A-Ha moment. Somewhere inside the self-inflicted fog, she had lost her confidence. Her intuition was so wrong about Jack; how could she have faith in her instincts at work? Caroline had always gone with her gut, and after Jack, she didn't trust it. But having just worked through it, she realized she hadn't been off about Jack. He was ambitious and self-centered from the start, which is what initially appealed to her. *Birds of a feather, as they say...* With two people obsessively driven, it was only a matter of time before one put their objectives above the other. Looking back, it was a miracle it took as long as it did. If it were hers and not Jack's goal within reach, would she have expected him to put his aspirations on hold to accommodate her? Maybe. But Caroline knew, without a doubt, she was incapable of turning a situation around to place undeserved blame on someone she loved. And that was the difference between them. That made her the bigger person.

Having cleaned the first closet of her mind, Caroline enjoyed the rush of a job well done and felt lighter than before. Mentally drained but content with the progress she'd made,

Caroline patted the journal in a silent "thank you". *I love you, Mom.* Suddenly energetic, she decided to collect more treasures for Saturday's wreath making, and with a young girl's heart, skipped into the cabin to change.

# Chapter XVIII

Caroline returned home from her walk to find Dan sitting on the steps next to a box. "Whatcha got?" she asked.

"The wreath supplies Emmy wanted from the store. She asked me to drop them off." Caroline sensed there was something more and patiently waited. After a pause, Dan came out with it. "Emmy told me about the journal and your conversation with Will."

Caroline started to assure him she wasn't trying to pry when he stopped her mid-sentence.

"I know that. But it brought back your family's incredible kindness. They stopped a screwed-up kid's world from spinning out of control, saved my relationship with my father, and gave me my mom. I only hope I made clear how much it all meant to me. How could I possibly have shown enough appreciation for all of that?"

"By being the stand-up guy you are and living a good life."

Dan kissed her on the cheek. "You know, when you first got here, I couldn't see the McMerritt in you, but I do now."

He grinned as a warm glow of pride crept over Caroline's face. "Humility becomes you. You should try it more often."

"Now you sound like Otis."

Laughing, Dan thanked her for the compliment and gave her a backward wave on his way back to his truck.

Emmy arrived Saturday morning to find Caroline at the picnic table, deep in thought, arranging and rearranging items in a circular shape. Quick to catch her friend's enthusiasm, She hurried to unpack the supplies. It took a couple of hours and a world of patience, but Caroline finally got the hang of wreath-making. Once she was ready to go, the friends decided to design their first creations for each other.

Surveying the finished products, the two ladies were quite proud of themselves. "If I may say so myself, Caroline, these are stunning, very artistic, and original. We should sell them at the store; I know we could get a pretty penny for them."

"Maybe in the future, but these are for us." Caroline handed Emmy her wreath inspired by Dan and Emmy's love. Its base, made of twigs, various lengths, and thicknesses, was adorned with feathers and wooden beads woven throughout on vines. A small bird's nest sat tucked in the corner. A sturdy, earthy foundation intertwined with an airy lightness and beauty. The beads represented the solid strength of their commitment, and the nest was their home. Emmy was beyond touched; Caroline had captured the very essence, the heart of her and Dan's relationship. Speechless, she hugged her friend tight in fond appreciation.

Emmy's wreath was an expression of Addisen Lake's charm. She'd woven yellow and blue tulle in and out of dark green boughs representing the sun, water, and forest to depict how the three intertwined together and created its natural beauty. Dried flowers and berries covered the lower left side portraying Caroline's new gardens and their growing friendship. A red satin bow tied at the end of the bouquet honored the cardinal. A gift she would cherish always, the wreath captured all the things in Addisen that Caroline held most dear. Her voice broke as she thanked Emmy.

Uncomfortable with the show of emotion, Caroline suggested they break for lunch. As the two friends enjoyed their grilled chicken salads, she ventured a question she'd been dying to ask. "So, what's Otis' story?"

"As in…?"

"All of it. It appears Otis spends most of his time puttering around the lake doing nothing, but he gets called away on business. Seems odd to me. There is no wife, so divorced? Never married? And why would he want to live up here alone, isolated?"

Emmy shot Caroline a perplexed look as if surprised by something. Appearing unsure of what to say, she hesitated a minute while Caroline sat back, arms crossed, and waited. Emmy finally seemed to decide what to share and started to fill in her cousin's blanks.

Otis, unlike her and Dan, lived at the lake year-round growing up. So, when it came time for college, he wanted the big city experience and went to NYU. Manhattan being the total opposite of Addisen, he was grateful his maternal grandfather lived in the city. The two had remained in touch through the years but were never exceptionally close. After Otis' mother's death, his grandfather, a widower, had closed himself off emotionally. Having built a sizeable empire, he enjoyed a luxurious but emotionally barren life. With Otis in the city and so many years passed, he allowed himself to open his heart again. The lonely elderly man grew very fond of his grandson, and Otis, thrilled to have a part of his mom alive, was eager to hear stories of her. Their bond was quick and unbreakable as if to make up for the lost time.

In his sophomore year, Otis met Clarice, and they instantly fell crazy in love. Clarice's family traveled in the same social circle as his grandfather, so she assumed Otis was among the Manhattan elite. It didn't take long for her to realize he was far from a socialite, but it only made her love him more. Otis, for his part, was completely taken with her. Beautiful, self-assured, and accustomed to a life of privilege, Clarice was a spitfire. Unafraid to stand up against anyone or anything to get what she wanted. She was also incredibly spoiled, which Otis didn't, or couldn't see.

Summers were the only time they were apart. Clarice went to the Hamptons and Otis to the lake. She dreamed of the day they would own a summer place in South Hampton, and he looked forward to the day they would make their home in Addisen. They were too naïve and too in love to see the writing on the wall.

In the spring of Otis's senior year, Clarice finally coerced him to go to the Hamptons for a long weekend. Otis hated every minute of it. He was appalled by the extravagant lifestyle and luxury, constant partying, and insincere smiles. But he was also aware of how comfortably Clarice fit in. Enough, so he didn't let his distaste show. Otis remained undeterred, convinced once Clarice spent time in Addisen, she'd succumb to its charm. They planned to spend a week at the lake after graduation.

The trip was a disaster from the start. While Clarice knew it would be a much different lifestyle to hers, she had pictured something akin to Kennebunkport, Maine, where the Bush family summered. A quaint but upscale seaside town with a casual but elite society. She was not prepared for some campground in the wilderness, as she called it. She couldn't believe her Otis revered such a place, much less expected her to live there. Addisen's effect on her was immediate and far from magical. She didn't even last the week. As much as she loved him, she absolutely would not live like this. As much as he loved her, he wouldn't live anywhere else. Outside of the insulated bubble college life provided, the inevitable was quick to happen. They parted ways, broken-hearted but lessons learned. Within two years, Clarice had married a real estate tycoon, and Otis was tucked in back home.

"He realized this place meant more to him than anything or anyone and that it takes a certain kind of woman to live out here. Up until now, he's managed to keep a lock on his heart."

Caroline ignored Emmy's not-so-subtle implication and raised eyebrows. "What about his business?"

Emmy continued the story. A year or so after Otis graduated, his grandfather was diagnosed with terminal cancer and told Otis he was leaving everything to him. His grandson said thank you but no, and suggested they set up nonprofits in honor of him, his wife, and Otis's mom. The grandfather agreed, but only if Otis would sit on the boards with a watchful eye. He also insisted Otis accept a generous gift to do with whatever he pleased and to allow him to pay off his college loans. All three stipulations were non-negotiable. Otis shook on it and used the gift to build his father the cabin of his dreams. The grandfather thrived on setting up the nonprofits and staffing them with the best in the business, and his cancer went into remission. Once everything was to his satisfaction, however, the disease returned, and he deteriorated quickly. Otis brought him to the lake to live out his time surrounded by peace and companionship.

"He will tell you the month spent living with his dad and grandfather under the same roof was the best of his life. Their talks and interactions, inspirational and heartfelt, left a lasting impression on him.

When he passed, Otis discovered his grandfather, despite agreeing not to, had left him a small trust fund in his will. Hes uses it to fund the camp and transportation for inner-city kids," Emmy concluded.

"Well, that explains where he disappears to on occasion. But if Otis gives it all away, how does he live?" Caroline asked.

Emmy swept her arm, encompassing their surroundings. "By owning all of this."

"Wait! You mean…?"

"Yep. Otis is an Addisen. I can't believe you didn't know!"

"He didn't offer his last name, and I never thought to ask."

Emmy continued. "This land and lake have been in his family for generations. His ancestor won it in a poker game when it was nothing but wilderness and a vision. Each generation took pride in the progress made by those before them and expanded on the dream. Addisen men have cleared the land for the town, campsites, and summer shacks through the years. Otis' great-grandfather and his brothers built the camp and carved out hiking trails. Along with his brothers, his grandfather built rental cabins and started to lease land for people to construct their own. Otis's dad upgraded the wells, winterized some of the rentals, and offered canoe and fishing gear by the day."

Emmy took a breath and ended the story. "When his father retired to Florida, he handed it all over to Otis, an only child. So far, Otis has restocked the lake with trout and bass, winterized the remaining cabins, and expanded equipment rentals to include jet skis and motorboats. It's a lot to oversee and a great deal of work. Especially trying to continue the tradition of doing much of the upkeep himself."

"Why doesn't he hire an overseer?"

"That is a question you'll have to ask him. I've spilled enough beans for now. Besides, I need to get some errands done, and you need to water the gardens."

With a quick hug, Emmy took off, and Caroline was left to process all she had learned. One thing she already knew for sure: Addisen Lake's ripples ran deep.

# Chapter XIX

When Otis still hadn't shown up a week later, Caroline was forced to admit it bothered her. She told herself it was only Charlie she missed but knew better. Now that Emmy had given her his history, Caroline was intrigued on top of the primal physical pull she felt towards him. Otis Addisen was turning out to be quite the enigma for her.

Unable to curb her curiosity, Caroline took the moped and headed counterclockwise for the other side of the lake. She figured Otis' father's dream cabin would be easy to find among the modest fishing structures. She was right. It was more like a log mansion. The chalet was built into a hill, with natural rock steps lined with hand-crafted stone walls leading down to the beach and a dock with a hydraulic boat lift. A boathouse sat off to the left. The entire lakeside façade was tinted glass, save for the deck that wrapped around the center of the house. Letting out a low whistle, Caroline parked the moped and climbed the stairs to peek inside. The lower level, a vast open space, was partitioned off with furniture creating separate areas. There was a home theater with reclining leather seats and an old fashion popcorn maker. A game space included a pool table, foosball, air hockey, pinball machine, and poker table. A fully equipped office faced the lake, and a kitchenette was tucked in the back. She assumed there was a bathroom somewhere. *It's the man cave of every male's dream.* Caroline climbed the deck stairs, and was presented with a breathtaking view.

The water sparkled in the sunlight like sequins, and the beaches, docks, and cabins appeared to dance around it in celebration. The woodland stood tall as if shielding it all from outside harm. Awe-inspiring is the word that came to her mind. It not only encompassed the natural beauty, but the accomplishments of generations as well. *An Addisen overlooking this view must experience an all consuming pride, and devotion akin to a parent gazing at their sleeping child – and I imagine they both evoke the same all-consuming devotion.* Snapping out of her reverie, she turned back to the house. Without the shade provided by the deck overhang, the glare made it difficult to see as much detail. She could see an open floor plan with a twenty-foot ceiling and a massive four-sided stone fireplace that commanded the middle space. Because of the sun, she couldn't make out what lay beyond the fireplace but had seen enough to know it would be spectacular.

Her curiosity sated, Caroline decided to take a ride around the lake. Learning Addisen's history gave her a new perspective, and she wanted to see it through enlightened eyes. She explored the corners of each gem the lake offered, picturing the different generations as they worked tirelessly to carve out their facet in the family jewel. Caroline marveled at the dedication, love of the land, and family pride it must have taken and now appreciated Addison for the extraordinary legacy it represented.

Hungry, she headed back to the cabin and received a warm welcome from a barking furball of joy. "Charlie, where have you been? I missed you!" The dog pranced around, then plopped down and rolled over so she could prove it with a belly rub. Laughing, she bent down to oblige him as Otis rounded the corner of the cabin.

"How far you've come, milady – from hiding behind a door in avoidance to belly rubs."

Caroline refused to take the bait. "You've been gone a while."

Otis raised his eyebrows. "You missed me too?"

"Don't flatter yourself. Why didn't you tell me you were an Addisen?" she asked, her tone harsher than intended.

"Maybe I was hoping to win you over with just my charm."

"First, you need to have some," she retorted.

A look crossed Otis's face, and Caroline realized she had landed punches, not jabs.

Shaking his head, Otis backed away. "So much for absence making the heart grow fonder." He called to Charlie. "Come on, boy, let's go home. I'm not up for a boxing match today."

As he headed for the skiff, Caroline was overcome by a need to stop him. With no time to analyze why she ran to stand between him and the boat. Otis closed the distance until their noses almost touched and stood staring at her. Out of breath, she followed her instincts and kissed him hard. The kind of kiss no man had ever denied her. Until now. Otis pulled away.

"No, no way." He made the motion of wiping dirt from his hands, a look of disgust on his face. Puzzled, she started to question him when he spoke. "I figured you had a tough heart, but for money? Always thought you had more pride than that."

Confused, it took Caroline a minute to grasp what he meant. *He thinks I'm making a play for him now because I know he has money.* She stared at him, too paralyzed with emotions to react. Rage, shock, hurt, and indignation all raced through her veins, setting her insides afire. After a long silent moment, her breathing stilled, and she regained control. She took a step back, and with a quiet "Goodbye, Otis," walked to the cabin, the blood pounding in her ears mixing with Charlie's whines.

Once alone, Caroline tried to chill out and piece together what had just happened. Analyzing the conversation, she began to see different nuances. When Otis thought she meant she'd missed him too, he didn't respond with his typical sarcasm. *Did I want to hint that I had? Yes. Maybe. I don't know.* Regardless, her bite back reset the tone. She hadn't intended to snap at him for not telling her he was an Addisen but realized now that's precisely what she did. Why? *Because I felt duped, misled.* It dawned on Caroline that Otis's reference to the quote had triggered her response to his leaving, alerted her that something was different. She panicked and, to stop him, went with a knee-jerk reaction: the kiss, to take command of the situation. *No – to stop him from walking away. Geez, This whole honest, self-awareness thing is exhausting!*

After reflecting, Caroline could see how he might've misconstrued things. After all, she had missed much herself. But did that excuse his automatic reflex to categorize her as a money-grabbing whore and a sellout? *Shields.* Emmy was right; they kept throwing up shields to protect themselves from one another. It was all too complicated. Best to let it and him go rather than make herself crazy trying to figure it out. *I have enough on my mental plate as it is.*

Caroline kept herself extra busy for the next few days, trying to keep her mind occupied. But no matter what she did, she couldn't stop thinking about him, couldn't focus on anything else. *It's because you always want what you can't have and see it as a challenge to win. Forget it. There's no prize to be had this time*, she told herself, hoping it would eventually sink in.

One evening Caroline had dozed off reading in the rocker and was jolted awake by a fist banging on the door. It was an enraged Otis. "I've got things to get off my chest, and you're going to listen!"

"You've got nothing to say that I want to hear! Leave me alone!"

Otis started banging harder, yelling to open it or he'd break it down.

"Someone's going to call the sheriff, you idiot!" Heart pounding and seeing red, she ripped the door open, her mouth poised to return his tirade. But one look at her, and Otis stopped mid-rant, clamped his mouth down on hers, and pulled her to him. His mouth never leaving hers, he kicked the door shut, and with all inhibition and pretense gone, they began clawing at each other's clothes. Caroline broke free from her jeans, and with Otis's still around his ankles, he hoisted her onto the table, her long legs wrapping around him, trapping him like prey. The dam that had held back the white-water rapids of their denied desire burst in a flood of fury, lust, and raw, primal coupling. It was as intense as it was swift. Panting and stunned, they broke apart and stared at each other like deer in headlights.

Feeling like a bowl of Jell-O, Caroline slid down onto a chair. "What the hell just happened?"

Shaking, Otis put his hands on his knees. "Damned if I know."

An awkward silence followed. Finally, able to pull himself together, Otis retrieved his pants from his ankles, handed Caroline her jeans, and without a word, let himself out. She heard him whistle for Charlie before all went quiet. Slipping into her jeans and hoping some fresh air would clear her head, she opened the door to find Otis and Charlie standing there.

"How do you feel about trying something a little more conventional?" he asked.

"You mean like a date?"

"Yeah."

"Are you sure?"

"No."

Neither was she. "How about Friday? I'll make dinner."

"You cook?"

She shook her head no."I make sandwiches."

"I eat sandwiches."

"Okay then, it's a date. Six o'clock?"

"Six it is. A date."

Caroline heard him say, "God help us all, Charlie," as they headed for the truck. She could not have agreed more.

# Chapter XX

W*hat. Have. I. Done?* Emotions were hitting Caroline's psyche with the force of a tsunami. A couple of months ago, she would have denied any feelings, considered it a challenge won and forgotten about the whole thing. But Caroline was no longer that woman. Not entirely, anyway. *Maybe this one matters?* No, she refused to believe that. She needed to talk this out with someone, but who? Typically, it would be Will, but there are certain things you can't discuss with your brother, and wild sex on the kitchen table with a guy who pisses you off is one of them. Never mind him helping her get the puzzle pieces of her mind and body's reaction to the whole thing to fit. Emmy would be of help there, but Otis being her cousin ruled her out. No, Caroline was on her own with this one. She made a cup of chamomile tea and sat down to sift through the debris herself.

The first thing she addressed was her feeling of relief. The physical tension created every time she and Otis interacted had built up more than she realized. Now that it was released, Caroline's body felt lighter, freed. The mental stress, however, had doubled and left her head feeling like a bowling ball. She admitted her attraction to him was no longer strictly physical. Should it be explored? With a chuckle, she acknowledged the upcoming date had already made that decision. Caroline concluded that, like it or not, this one might have the potential to matter, and there was only one way to find out. What she would do if he did, she hadn't a clue. *Baby steps, Mom, right?* Caroline decided to take the journal to bed and let the words of her mom's memories lull her to sleep.

*It's been four years since we last summered at the lake. Two kids and living in Connecticut takes money. Until Bill climbed the corporate ladder, I had to go to work, or we had to rent the cabin. For us, it was an easy decision. Oh, but how I missed Addisen! It's so good to be back, and our place is in tip-top shape. Mr. Addisen was gracious enough to keep an eye on things and open and close the cabin each season. His sister even tended my gardens, and she must have quite the green thumb because they are gorgeous. I'll have to make them a casserole and pie to thank them.*

*I love my daughter, but she is a handful. Today Will and Caroline were ankle-deep in the lake, collecting minnows in a bucket. I watched from the porch as Caroline turned and started walking further into the water and over her head. In the second it took me to run out, Will had pulled her up, choking and sputtering. She wanted to see what it felt like to be a fish. While I wanted to throttle her, Will calmly explained to her fish "breathe" differently and to ask questions before acting next time. Caroline hugged him and promised she would. Later, my son shared his logic with me. "If you tell sister she can't, she will. If you tell her no, she doesn't hear. She wants to figure out everything about everything herself. It's just her way, is all." Thank goodness for Will and his understanding of her. He's right, of course. Curiosity drives Caroline along with a need to know. I will remember my son's words when guiding her. But Lord, I do hope she develops some common sense; sooner rather than later.*

---

*When I told Bill what happened, he laughed and told me I worry too much. How can I expect a five-year-old spitfire to think things through? When I reminded him that Will had always done so, he made an excellent point. Will experiences life by thoughtful observation and asking questions. Caroline rushes headlong into life to experience everything first-hand. They have opposite temperaments. Agreed. I remind myself of the promise I made when Donna died; I would accept the people I love for who they are. I need to try harder to process life as Caroline does to better understand her. Then I can teach her to set boundaries, to think some before leaping, as it applies to her way, not mine. Even at her young age, I know my daughter is not made for the same path I chose in life. But that doesn't make it wrong, just different. I must change the way I parent her. Make adjustments to guide her in the best way for her.*

*How we spun two completely different children from the same cloth escapes me, but I'm grateful they are both ours.*

A few more entries followed about "lake life," as her mom called it: walks, barbeques, bonfires, and such. A mention of the time Caroline got covered in poison ivy, crawling through the woods looking for rabbits and the ensuing rash and drama. She couldn't understand why the animals didn't catch it, but she did. And why shouldn't a person scratch an itch if it made it feel better? Caroline smiled, thinking, *I still applied that logic to life, usually to my detriment.*

The journal's following years were more of the same: a mixture of family fun, restful days, and tranquil evenings laced with Caroline's antics. Their mom was so proud the day she found Will teaching her to swim. Caroline remembered it well. Will had caught up to her running down the dock to jump off and suggested she learn to swim first. One of the many times her brother had saved her from herself. *He still does,* she mused. Mom recorded her fall from the tree, her feelings on the matter, and

Will's doting on his injured little sister. Though her love for her daughter was ever-present in her writings, Caroline could see through the years that her mother's words of exasperation began to intertwine with patience and finally became understanding. Her mom being of a different mindset, Caroline could appreciate the effort it took for her mother to accept her fearlessness and head-strong ways and still love her unconditionally. *You aced it, Mom.* She laid a loving hand on the journal. *And still are*. Feeling drowsy, she was about to put the diary down when an entry made that impossible to do.

*Push has come to shove. I must talk to Bill tonight. He's asked Will to go fishing tomorrow, just the two of them, and I know it's time to have 'the talk.' So often, I've wanted to share my gut feeling with Bill but didn't know how to begin the conversation. I still don't, but I will tonight. I need to, for my husband's sake as well as my son's. I pray I can find the right words.*

---

*I needn't have worried. Bill had the same feeling and had made the same observations as me. Will's lack of interest in girls and his discomfort when friends talked about nothing else. Our son becoming increasingly less social and more withdrawn, even at home. Bill worries it is due to confusion and, God forbid, shame. If our hunch is correct and Will is gay, he needs to know we love and support him. Not to mention hormonal urges and sex are a conundrum for any teen, regardless of sexual orientation, and need to be discussed. Bill feels the time is right, and I agree. I'm reminded, once again, of how well I married.*

---

*Will came flying through the door after fishing and hugged me so tight I could barely breathe. He was laugh-crying and Bill stood behind him, grinning with a thumbs up. When he finally pulled away, Will stared into my eyes with such love that I melted from the inside out. Lost for words, I put his face in my hands and told him I loved him. "I know, Mom, thank you," he said and ran off to find Caroline to help clean the fish. Our boy was back. I closed my eyes and thanked Donna. All these years later, my friend's teachings are still with me. Without them, things could have turned out very differently for our family.*

*So that explains why Will had always been comfortable with his homosexuality, so confident and self-assured,* Caroline thought. Once again, she appreciated how fortunate they'd been in the parent department.

# Chapter XXI

Caroline spent the day Friday alternating between excitement and dread, equally concerned things would go well or they would not. To keep her mind from short-circuiting, she weeded and watered the gardens, filled the bird feeders, then went to town to get what was needed for dinner.

Caroline had never taken an interest in cooking, nor had she ever needed to. Her lifestyle was one of either fine dining or, on late nights at the office, take-out. She did make a decent tomato basil soup and a gourmet grilled cheese of sorts, which would be dinner. Caroline added a strawberry shortcake to the menu, spotting juicy strawberries at the farmer's stand and figuring she could handle cracking open a tube of biscuits. She stopped at the store to complete her list and was relieved to see Dan's truck and not Emmy's. Caroline knew Emmy would sense something was up and wasn't ready to have the conversation. She picked up the remaining items and headed home.

Once the soup was made and the table set, it was time to concentrate on herself. Caroline soaked in the tub, moisturized, applied minimal makeup and a light perfume. Deciding on leggings, a low-cut camisole, and a sheer flowing over-blouse, she was happy with the right amount of sexy looking back from the mirror. Now all that was left to do was wait and not overthink things. The former was doable, the latter not so much.

Fortunately, it wasn't a long wait. Answering the knock, Caroline opened the door to a transformed Otis. He wore a white linen button-down shirt, sleeves rolled up and opened at the neck, paired with khaki pants, both tailored and expensive. Italian loafers with no socks completed the look, and he wore it well. Very well. Otis and Caroline gave each other the once over and chorused, "You clean up nicely," breaking the awkward silence. Sitting at attention beside him, a freshly groomed Charlie held a bouquet of wildflowers gently in his mouth. Caroline ushered them in, took the flowers from Charlie, cooing her thanks and fussing over him, and the pup quickly returned to his frisky self. With everyone comfortably back to themselves, they settled into a pleasant evening. Caroline and Otis bantered as always, but a playfulness had replaced the bite. Otis raved about her tomato basil soup while Charlie snubbed his nose at the peanut butter bread, insisting on his own grilled cheese. Caroline burnt the biscuits, so they had a strawberry shortcake without the cake, but no one complained.

After dinner, Charlie curled up in front of the fire, snoring contently, while the couple talked endlessly. They shared experiences of their childhood, college, and love lost.

Discussing Jack and Clarice in-depth brought them insight as to why they were so abrasive towards one other. Otis explained that he felt his attraction to Caroline growing and needed to beat it back. "I guess I did it by putting you down." No way he was getting hung up on another Manhattan beauty, full of both fire and ice, he elaborated. One heartbreak was enough. For Caroline, Otis's sarcasm and take-downs cut too close to Jack's final accusations. She had equated haughty and uppity to self-centered and cold, unfair criticism she vowed no man would hurl at her again. She felt Otis needed to be put in his place.

"Our pasts put different faces on us," Caroline observed.

Otis agreed. "I saw Clarice, and you saw Jack."

*Protective shields.* Caroline shared Emmy's previous observations of their behavior and what she thought it meant.

"Looks like her intuition was on target," Caroline said.

Otis nodded. "It usually is."

With the core issue recognized, both were hopeful they could move forward as Otis and Caroline.

They exchanged travel stories, bringing the breathtaking trips to life and sharing a laugh at the disasters. Switching to politics, Otis expressed he was surprised but pleased to hear Caroline was a liberal. Being a well-to-do, big corporate city dweller, he told her he had assumed she was a staunch conservative but instead learned how passionate she was about gay and women's rights.

They compared city versus rural living, the best music, their favorite authors, and movies. After shared opinions on different religions, they discovered both firmly believed in 'to each his own.' The couple was ready to begin solving the world's problems when Charlie stirred and needed to go out. It was only then they realized how late it was. Caroline walked them to the door and, standing so close that only heat was between them, their eyes locked in a longing stare. Showing the utmost control, Otis whispered a "thank you for the evening" and kissed her ever so softly on the lips, gently tugging on her lower lip as he pulled away. It was as sweet as it was sensual, and the combination left Caroline off-balance and wanting more. Missing him before the door was closed, she knew for certain this one mattered. She started turning out the lights when a text came through on her phone. "Dinner at my place Sunday?" Relieved she wasn't the only one sinking fast, she typed "I look forward to it" and was a little frightened by how much she meant it.

No longer used to late nights, Caroline slept until noon Saturday. With a sigh, she took her coffee onto the porch to listen to her voicemails and clear the full mailbox. It was time. She had ignored her countless emails since leaving NYC, so she knew they were beyond tackling. *Oh well, they'll have to settle for one out of two,* she thought as she sat down. Caroline had refused to help PG&G with clients during the forced hiatus to prove her worth. She felt the firm decided to do business without her for a while, and any hardship it caused they deserved. She had made good use of the time, but that didn't take the sting out of their disloyalty.

Maci's many messages made clear the company viewed the time off as a gift, a reprieve, and was increasingly annoyed at her silence. Caroline sensed PG&G was close to issuing an ultimatum and didn't know how she'd respond. The fact that was even in question proved things had shifted inside of her. Initially, she had ignored all company contacts out of vindictiveness, but as weeks passed, had realized the need to step away for the journey of self-discovery. And now? Caroline wasn't sure what self she had been or was in the process of being. One thing she did know for sure: she was different. Deciding to leave that bag to unpack for a later time, she went for a swim.

An hour later, limbs aching but feeling rejuvenated, she laid on a floating raft, drying off. The sun's warmth, the breeze's caress on her skin, and the gentle rocking of the waves combined to lull her into a dream-like state. It was the same soothing feeling she experienced as a toddler when held by her mother. Her mom would cuddle her close, her breath softly fluttering on Caroline's cheek as she sang in a hushed tone, rocking lightly. The memory, long forgotten, brought a rush of contentment and a sense of safety to Caroline. She realized that, if fully appreciated, nature offered the same tranquility to an adult that parents provide in childhood. *Well, at least some of it; the rest you have to develop on your own, she reasoned.*

She spent the remainder of the afternoon and evening watering the gardens, chatting with Will on the phone, and re-reading her favorite chapters of *Little Women*. It occurred to her not only had she conquered the art of relaxing but, had learned to enjoy it. Unwinding was something she never thought necessary, much less attainable. Could she return to her frenetic life in NYC now that she knew the benefits of a day of quiet solitude? Could she find a way to carve out time in that whirlwind pace to regroup occasionally? That notion made her laugh out loud. *Of course not.* Caroline knew to stay viable in that world, a person needed to be on, twenty-four seven. She had crushed many who had made the mistake of letting up for even a minute. But Caroline also knew a lifetime of her summer experience would turn her brain to mush and kill her spirit; she needed more to thrive. Determined not to ruin the glow of the day, Caroline turned in early, leaving yet another piece of mental luggage unpacked.

# Chapter XXII

Caroline spent Sunday morning collecting treasures for wreath making. Remembering the intimate detail and thought she and Emmy put into each other's gift made her smile. She tried to mentally create a wreath portraying her and Otis. *It would be a tangled mess of confusion and fear, adorned with raw sexuality, and, after Friday night, laced with tenderness and friendship*. No, best to let that be, for now.

Otis wasn't picking her up until six o'clock, so Caroline had time to kill before getting ready. She took a book of poetry to the hammock and immersed herself in the beautiful poems to keep from overthinking. It worked, and before she knew it, it was time to get dressed. Opting once again for casual-chic with a touch of sexy and minimal make-up, Caroline was ready early and waited on the porch for her date. She was surprised when Otis pulled up in the boat wearing cargo shorts and a sweat-stained t-shirt. Grinning sheepishly, he explained there was an issue at the camp that took longer than expected. Not wanting to be late, he opted to pick her up first and clean up later. Sensing the need to be a gentleman, Charlie refrained from jumping into the water and greeted her dry from the boat. After the trip across the lake, Otis docked the skiff and held his hand out for Caroline. As he helped her ashore, she inhaled his manliness and found it intoxicating. Unaccustomed to the scent of a man after a day's physical labor, she decided it was not an entirely unpleasant odor.

Otis made sure she was comfortably settled on the deck and went to shower. Within a half-hour, he returned with a bottle of sparkling water, smelling cleaner but just as manly. *No cologne for this guy and none needed,* she thought. Otis's hair, still damp, was pulled back in a bun, and his skin shone from its recent scrubbing. His feet were bare, and the tight fit of his jeans accentuated his manhood. Caroline found herself struggling to keep her eyes on the view over the railing. As they appreciated the sunset in comfortable silence, the sparks between them darted around like hundreds of fireflies. When dusk settled in, Otis stood and pulled her up within a breath of him. They lingered there, eyes burning with anticipated desire. He ran his thumb across her lips, sending the fireflies into a frenzy. Otis shook his head as if to clear it and whispered, seemingly to himself, "Not yet." To disenchant the moment, he quickly offered her the fifty-cent tour.

He took Caroline's hand and led her into the house, unaware she had seen most of it. His love and pride in the home were evident as he pointed out the family's workmanship. His dad's craftmanship with wood shone through in the beauty of the staircases and banisters, and the magnificent fireplaces showcased Otis's expertise. The rooms Caroline hadn't seen were even more elegant than she'd imagined. Both guest bedrooms had a sitting area and private bath, equipped with a soaking tub, walk-in rain shower, and heated floor.

The master suite was impressive, to say the least. A wall of floor-to-ceiling windows overlooked the lake, giving Caroline the heady sensation of being a bird sitting high in a nest. Cozy chairs and floor pillows were clustered about, creating intimate nooks to enjoy the panoramic beauty. A California king-sized bed sat on a platform opposite the wall of windows. Otis had crafted a stone waterfall that lined the wall behind it, complete with colored dimming lights. A three-sided fireplace was strategically placed to the right side of the room, providing enjoyment from all areas. Caroline noticed there was no desk or TV. Otis explained, he, like his father, believed there were plenty of places to work and watch entertainment. A bedroom should be a sanctuary, a place to decompress. Nodding towards a built-in bookcase lined with books, Caroline commented he must like to read.

"Those belonged to my mom. She was an avid reader and read most mornings and before bed. Dad liked having them in his private quarters so he could begin and end each day with her memory."

Her spine tingled when Otis mentioned his mom's most treasured book was *Little Women*. Caroline had forgotten it was her childhood favorite until recently when she rediscovered it at the cabin. Before the diary, Caroline would've said it was just a coincidence, but now she knew better.

The master bath completed the suite. It was an immense space, with an open stone shower (Otis's handiwork), a double vanity, and his and her water closets. An oversized jetted tub was tucked into a private corner with a spectacular view of the forest. Her head full of fantasies of what lay ahead, Caroline blushed when she saw how intently Otis was watching her. Fearful he could read her thoughts, she was happy when they moved down to the kitchen.

The chef's kitchen was state of the art, equipped with every high-end appliance, gadget, and cookware imaginable. When Caroline teased it was not a typical bachelor's setup, Otis just shrugged. "I like to cook; it relaxes me."

She sat at the island and watched as he expertly prepared their meal. A fresh green salad dressed in a homemade lemon vinaigrette to start, followed by a mushroom and shallot risotto paired with pan-seared scallops. Caroline was thoroughly enjoying herself until Otis reached down and lifted a bottle of wine from the wine cooler. She and time both froze, and everything began to move in slow motion. Her eyes never left the bottle, and her mouth went dry. *A drink. Surely one drink won't hurt. Yes, it will! You're an alcoholic. But does wine even count as alcohol? You know it does!* She vaguely heard Otis's voice fade in and out as she fought her inner battle. Something about Sauvignon Blanc pairing well with seafood. *One. Just one. NOOOOOO!* Otis was describing the wine's grapefruit overtones… *Yes, damn it. I will be fine! No, You won't. Yes. I. Will.* Otis turned around, the uncorked bottle ready to pour, and went still. Caroline knew her contorted face, and focused stare on the bottle, told him the story. He gave her a moment before calling her back. "Caroline," he said softly.

*No, no more!* I *want to be fully present tonight. And for life.* It was an epiphany moment, and with it, Caroline passed her first test.

She blinked, cleared her throat, and in a clear, determined voice, said, "I don't drink, but you go ahead." It was a statement, not a mere comment.

Otis gave her a long look, smiled broadly, and tucked the bottle away. "I'm good. Sparkling water it is."

Freshly baked cannoli filled with ricotta and chocolate, served with expresso, completed the decadent meal.

Caroline leaned back in the chair with a sigh. "I've eaten in the best restaurants in NYC, and that meal tops them all."

It was Otis's turn to redden. "Why, thank you, milady. I'm glad you enjoyed it."

Caroline cocked her head to one side. "I always hated when you called me that, and now I kind of like it. I think it's the tone." Caroline leaned over and kissed him softly on the lips. "You were quite the sarcastic jerk."

"And you the haughty witch," he said as he took her hand and led the way upstairs.

They spent hours exploring every inch of each other's bodies, their mouths and hands finding sweet spots that ignited arousal and sensations neither had ever experienced before. They made love on the bed, in the shower, on the pillows, in the jacuzzi, and back to bed, each time discovering more ways to pleasure one another to new climactic heights. They surrendered themselves with total abandonment and complete trust; body, heart, and mind, fully embracing their newfound utopia. Finally exhausted, the pair collapsed in a tangle of limbs and fell into a deep sleep, knowing they had reached a profound intimacy few ever achieved.

# Chapter XXIII

The smell of bacon frying enticed Caroline from her sweet dreams. The night before lingered, filling her senses and making her stretch like a contented cat. Her skin still hummed from his touch, and her nerve endings tingled, remembering his expert tongue. Her lips, swollen from their love-making, could taste his kisses and the salt of his sweat. The musky smell of their sex floated up from the sheets, and she purred at the memory of him moving inside her.

Caroline's stomach growled, bringing her back to the present, and she searched for something to wear. Finding a pair of Otis's sweatpants, she pulled the drawstring tight, threw on a flannel shirt, and followed her nose to the kitchen. Otis, shirtless and wearing pajama bottoms, had his back to her scrambling eggs. Caroline paused to enjoy the view and the warm stirring it caused within her.

She filled two mugs of coffee, gave his shoulder a playful nip, and set one down next to the chef. “Black, just how you like it.”

Grinning, Otis turned the burners off and gave her a deep, penetrating kiss that almost made them forget breakfast. Almost. Starved from their nighttime adventures, they sat at the island, inhaling eggs, bacon, and grilled bagels. Stomachs full, they were chatting over a second cup of coffee when Emmy burst in.

“Hi Cuz, I’m dropping off the…”

Taking in the scene rendered her speechless for all of two seconds before she started singing, “I knew it! I just knew it,” and jumped around the kitchen with Charlie. Too happy to contain herself, Emmy gave them both a quick hug before rushing out the door with an ear-to-ear grin and a wave. Otis called out for her to wait, but she was already dancing down the stairs. The couple shared a shy smile at her enthusiasm.

“Looks like Emmy approves,” Caroline said.

“And Charlie,” he said, nodding towards the dog curled up at her feet.

Seeming as unwilling to let her go as she was to leave, Otis asked her to join him on his day’s business, and she readily agreed. Caroline could tell he was surprised but pleased when she told him learning his family’s history had led her to explore Addisen through a different lens. How she now appreciated the contributions of each generation, the hard work and heart it took, their pride evident. It made her see Addisen in a new light.

Touched, Otis wrapped her in a bear hug. Caroline started to kiss his neck, and reluctantly he held her at arms' length.

"Work. First, I have to work."

He suggested Caroline take the truck home to change, and he and Charlie would pick her up in the boat after showering. But Charlie had his own plan, and as soon as Caroline opened the door, he bolted for the truck. Giggling, she opened the passenger side door and heard Otis yell, "So much for man's best friend," as the dog hopped in.

Within the hour, all three were in the skiff, skimming across the lake. Otis waved to fishermen he recognized and stopped to chat up those he did not. After some pleasantries, he asked to see their fishing license, and most had them. Otis requested those who didn't to stash their poles and enjoy other activities the lake offered. He pointed out to the stubborn few who gave him a hard time that he owned the property and could have them removed legally.

When Caroline mentioned that couldn't be good for business, Otis explained, "The revenue from license fees goes back into the fisheries and supports the conservation and stocking programs of the state. I have an obligation, as a landowner, to make sure my guests do their part."

Caroline couldn't argue with that. He added that stocking the lake with fish was his idea, and he was committed to managing and maintaining it responsibly.

"If I'm not diligent and allow over-fishing, the demand will drain the supply, and I'll have an empty lake."

When he told her the cost of stocking fish and the time it took to mature, she could see the logic in fighting against and losing a few unlicensed anglers.

Otis covered more ground in a day than Caroline thought possible; she couldn't believe she ever thought he was a deadbeat. He toured each area thoroughly, looking for issues that needed attention. He fixed a plumbing problem at the campground, replaced a window in a rental cabin, and sat in for the final interviews for next year's camp counselors. The last stop was the rental hut to change the oil in the jet skis and look at a damaged boat a guest had run aground. Caroline was envious of Otis's rapport with his staff and the pride they took in their work. They worked as a team for a common goal; their community. *No conniving or backstabbing here,* she thought.

With the day's work done, Otis headed full-throttle towards Caroline's. She didn't need to ask why. Her place was closer, and they were both aching to release the passion they had kept contained for hours. Laughing, they raced like teenagers towards the cabin but only made it as far as the outdoor shower before losing control. Stripped down within seconds, his mouth hungrily on hers, Otis hoisted Caroline about his waist, and her legs wrapped around him like a Python, forcing him deep within her. Their lovemaking was feverish and intense, as if the only way to sate their need was to devour one another whole. Breathless, Otis lowered Caroline to the ground and turned on the water. They soaped one another down, relishing each other's touch and the sensual, silky feel of the soap moving across their skin. Once the hot water was gone, they grabbed her parents' old terrycloth robes and headed inside. Caroline opened the fridge, expecting it to be bare, but found two plates heaped with pot roast and all the fixings, ready for the microwave. Otis chuckled as he handed her a note he found on the table.

*I thought you guys might be hungry after an exhaustive night and a busy day of work. Enjoy, Emmy :)*

"How did she know we were together all day and would end up here?"

"Easy. The Addisen gossip grapevine and the direction it crawled around the lake made your place our logical ending point."

"No privacy then? The word is out?"

"Afraid so, milady. We'll be the big news until something else comes along. Probably in a day or two."

"Alas, fame is so fleeting," she said with a wry smile.

The couple ate in compatible silence then settled in front of the fire. Caroline chose her well-worn copy of *Little Women* to read and Otis one of her father's fishing magazines. Feeling sorry for Charlie all alone on the floor, Caroline curled up beside him, and it wasn't long before she fell asleep. Dog hair tickling her nose and Otis spooning behind her, snoring softly in her ear, made her stir sometime during the night. Sandwiched between their two heartbeats, a feeling of love and being loved overcame her, and with a sigh, she dozed back off.

From that day on, one was rarely seen without the other two.

# Chapter XXIV

Weeks later, sitting on the porch swing after dinner, Otis mentioned he had to go to the city for a couple of days. The thought of NYC made Caroline cringe. She knew things were coming to a head with PG&G, and she had avoided it as long as she could. Otis wrapped his arm around her shoulders and pulled her close. Sitting with her arms around his waist and legs draped over his lap, she told him her angst over the imminent decision she was facing. Caroline felt his body tighten with dread, but he listened without judgment or pressuring her to stay. Ultimately, it was her choice, and only she knew what was best for her. When he said as much, she started to cry.

"But that's just it. I don't. I've always known who I was and what was suitable for me. But I've changed being here. And now there's you – us – and –"

Otis cut her off. "Shhh, you will figure it out."

He led her to the water's edge and gently undressed her. With her naked skin bathed in the moonlight, she did the same for him. Otis asked her to close her eyes, and when she hesitated, he lightly placed his hand over them. "Trust me, Caroline."

Taking both her hands in his, Otis gradually backed into the water. Caroline felt the water swallowing her slowly as his thumbs caressed the tops of her hands in reassuring circles. Otis tightened his grip as he walked them in over their heads, pulling her to him, and just as she needed a breath, steadily brought them back to shoulder depth. Holding her like a child, he spun around and around until she lost all sense of balance and equilibrium. Without warning, Otis suddenly dropped to his knees, lifting her safely over his head. Never once did she feel in danger.

Her eyes still closed, she allowed him to guide her to shore and opened them only when he swaddled her in a beach towel and carried her to the cabin. Otis laid her on the bed, tucked her in, and tenderly kissed her forehead.

"I will never let you fall. And I will never drop your heart."

With that, he turned to go, leaving Caroline even more confused and suddenly very lonely. I *do trust him. I believe him. And after only a couple of months. Why doesn't that set my warning bells ringing?* She rolled over, trying to clear her head. *Because you can't fake what we have. I'm no rookie; I would know.* Caroline flipped to her stomach. *I swore I'd never do it again. What happened? The real deal happened. Otis happened.* She tossed and turned through the night, no less clear about what to do for all her lost sleep.

Emmy stopped by around eight in the morning with her signature smile and plate of muffins. “I know Otis left this morning and figured we could catch up.” A look of concern crossed her face. “You look like hell. What’s wrong?” Caroline, unable to argue the point, agreed and told her it was a long story.

“For you, I’ve got all day. Let’s hear it.”

Caroline shared it all with her friend. That for the first time in her life, she felt confused about who she was and unsure of what she wanted or needed in life. About her fear of not knowing and the anxiety of so much inner change in such a short time. Was the shift real or simply adjusting to a different circumstance? Was she putting off the return to her city life out of fear she had lost her edge or drive? So many questions. Then there was Otis and the swift all-consuming emotions he brought to the mix.

“I do not know where to start, and that scares the bejesus out of me.”

“It’s a lot. I’ll give you that. But putting it off is no longer an option. It sounds like you’re about to lose your job. Not to mention your sanity. You need to sit down and have a therapy session with yourself, figure it out as best you can, and decide. Remember, no decision is irreversible; no choice has to be permanent.”

Emmy was right. Caroline gave her friend a grateful hug and decided today had to be the day. She grabbed a cup of tea and sat on the swing. It was time to unpack and organize the mess she'd been avoiding in the storage unit called her mind.

Caroline knew she was different than when she first arrived in Addison. Softer, more accessible, calmer. More patient and less volatile. Could the change be temporary due to the laid-back lifestyle? No, she didn't think so. She knew her mom's journal and friendship with Emmy were significant factors in her transformation, and had to be a permanent part of her now. Reading the diary had brought her mother's experiences, innermost feelings, and wisdom to life. They opened Caroline's heart and mind to friendship, and love, brought her strength and a new perspective. She now knew of her mom's effort to embrace her for who she was and parent her accordingly. It was time for Caroline to receive and welcome her mother's guidance in adulthood, and to put to good use the lessons and insights her mother provided so eloquently through her words.

Emmy. Her first real friend. So different from the Caroline that first arrived in Addisen, yet they quickly developed a kinship. Without knowing of her mom and Donna's swift bond, Caroline would never have been susceptive to the idea, much less trusted the connection. *Yet another gift you've given me, Mom.*

*Otis. What about Otis?* Caroline knew deep in her core this thing between them was different, exceptional. The strength of their bond, with such intensity in so little time, was extraordinary. A once in a lifetime connection. Could she leave and chance losing it? The ache she felt at his absence, even though it had been less than twenty-four hours, told her how difficult it would be. In the light of day, she pieced together why and how she so willingly gave herself to him. Again, it was the journal. Her mother's entries of the love her parents shared brought home how it was supposed to be. All in, not competitive or supportive only when convenient, as with Jack. It wasn't about falling for a suit full of ambition or a particular type, but for what lies within. *Receptive, not judgmental.* She and Otis needed time to develop, but she instinctively knew what they shared was genuine. *I'm learning, Mom…*

After struggling for hours, her heart battling her mind, she finally reached a conclusion. She was a firecracker all her life, always goal-oriented, even before her hectic win-at-all-cost lifestyle in NYC. It's what led her to that way of life and why she was so successful at it. Could she still be aggressive and viciously ambitious enough to succeed? *Do I even want to be?* There was only one way to find out. It came down to her being one way all her life versus another for mere months. She had made her decision. Caroline went in to call Will.

Otis got back late the next day, ran home to grab Charlie, and was at Caroline's by sunset. Watching them bound out of the truck towards her, all enthusiasm and excitement melted her to tears. *How can I possibly leave them?* One look at her face, and Otis stopped short.

"You're going back."

"I have to, I need to see…"

Caroline was crying hard as Otis walked to her and put a finger to her lips.

With tears rolling down his cheeks, he held her close.

"I hate it, but I get why."

With a confused Charlie whining at the celebration's abrupt end, they headed inside. Unable to eat, they sat on the couch staring at nothing, afraid to speak.

Finally, Otis asked, "When?"

"Will is picking me up tomorrow. If I'm not behind my desk Monday morning, PG&G will terminate me."

Otis cleared his throat and took a shaky breath. "I guess I should go so you can pack."

"No, please! Stay with me tonight. It will be a while before I can get back."

*How am I going to do this? How can I leave?* she thought. As if reading her mind, Otis gave her a smile.

"You are doing what you need to do."

*Is he being supportive or nonchalant?* Caroline silently wondered. Aloud, she asked, a little haughtily, "Am I?"

"Apparently, yes," he bit back with a hint of sarcasm.

They stared at one another briefly, then chorused, "Protective shields," with a sad smile.

"We haven't acted that way towards one another since replacing Jack and Clarice's faces with our own," Caroline said. "Why now?"

"Because we feel vulnerable again. And we're afraid of losing us," Otis said. "That the spell will be broken, and the intensity will wane once you leave."

Caroline shivered. *Please don't let that happen, s*he sent out to the universe.

They went to bed, and after making love tenderly, as if afraid to break something fragile, they clung to one another and rocked themselves to sleep.

Sometime later that night, Caroline's senses were stirred to life by soft caresses exploring her body and kisses fluttering across her skin, light as feathers. She softly groaned as they became more impassioned to meet her deepening arousal. Bringing her to the edge, Otis entered her slowly, with purpose, and covering her mouth with his, plunged them both into a free fall of erotic sensations. Untethered by egos, a oneness engulfed them, creating an emotional nirvana all their own. Gone was the earlier sadness, replaced by the promise of an unspoken vow. *The spell would not be broken.*

Caroline woke with the sun to find Otis had gone and a note resting on the nightstand.

*Sorry to leave while you were sleeping, milady. Charlie sucks at goodbyes.*

She read between the lines. *You guys aren't the only ones.* Her heart was heavy with tears, but still, she felt too sad to cry.

Caroline packed a bag of her personal items, cleaned out the fridge, and emptied the trash. She called Emmy to tell her of her decision and to thank her for everything.

"As much as I'll miss you, I understand the decision and the reasoning behind it," she said. "At least now you're pointed in a direction and can work through it from there. When do you leave?"

"This morning. Will is on his way now."

"Have you told Otis?"

"Of course, last night."

Hearing Caroline's voice crack, Emmy promised to look after him. "You need to do what you have to do."

"You are the best friend I've ever had, Emmy. I love you. I miss you already."

Emmy told her the same. "And Caroline? Please take care of yourself. Be mindful of the rat race and its trappings. Don't fall victim to your old demons."

Caroline promised to stay aware and hung up before emotions overtook sense.

Caroline watered the gardens to busy herself, proud of how they were filling in and so healthy. "Emmy will take good care of you too, I promise," she told them, then locked the cabin and sat on the porch swing to wait for Will. She took her mom's journal from the bag at her feet and held it close to her chest. Too upset to read it, just having it near eased her pain. When Will arrived, his jaw dropped as he surveyed the property's transformation. "Sis, you've worked miracles! The gardens look as good as they did when Mom was alive. She would be thrilled and so proud of you."

*She is, for so many reasons, Caroline thought.* "The gardens aren't the only thing that grew this season, Will. I'll tell you all about it on the way home. Come on, let's get going." *Before I chicken out.*

The last thing she saw as they pulled away was the cardinal perched on the porch rail.

# Chapter XXV

Caroline, quiet at first, started to talk the further they got from Addisen. She filled Will in on Otis, Emmy, the gardens maturing, her newfound love of nature, the history of Addisen, wreath making, and the cardinal. She looked over to find her brother grinning at her.

"You sure you're my sister? Gardening, dogs, history, a special guy, a girlfriend, spiritualism? It doesn't sound like the Caroline I worry about all the time. Don't get me wrong, I love it, but what happened?"

As she'd done from the time she could talk, Caroline shared everything with her brother. She told him of the year-long anger and frustration she had felt with herself and life, something she used alcohol to keep from facing. How she suffered the wrenching withdrawal symptoms when first arriving in Maine and finding the journal had helped her survive. The diary eventually opened her eyes to the value of friendship and love, allowing her to experience both for the first time and the lessons it taught of how nature could bring peace if you allow it to embrace you.

"The transformation started with the journal and snowballed from there," she concluded.

"Sounds to me like it started with you and a willingness to do some soul searching."

"Maybe. But let's remember I had to be forced to do it."

"You were forced to take a timeout; the decision to use it wisely was your choice."

"Was it? Or was it some divine intervention requested by Mom? The journal makes it clear she was always concerned about my fiery temperament. And I was on a destructive path."

"And now?"

"Sober as a recovering alcoholic can be." She shared the moment of reckoning at Otis's and how she came down on the right side. "I'm one for one," she said with a shaky laugh.

"You have the strength of an Amazon Queen. You'll be okay."

*I hope he's right...*"Heading back to the pressure and chaos will prove challenging, I'm sure. The ultimate test of my resolve."

Will assured her his money was on her. "You have never failed at something you set out to do, so no reason to believe you'll start now."

She gave him a grateful smile. *What do people do without a Will?*

Caroline explained the inner turmoil she was dealing with and the fear of combining who she'd always been with who she had become.

"Sis, you are you. Just because you've evolved, or transformed, or whatever, doesn't change that. What it does affect is how you approach life, your view of people and things, how you conduct yourself in situations."

"What if I can't do my job now or don't relate to who I've always been?"

"What if you find you don't want to?"

"What will I do?"

"You'll figure it out."

"Baby steps," they chorused with a smile.

Hector was at the apartment and greeted her with a kiss on each cheek and a hug. He was so ecstatic to see her he forgot to say hi to Will.

"Ahhhh, Helloooo…"

Laughing, Hector gave him a quick kiss and told him not to be so needy. In a whirlwind of sentences, he told her the cleaning crew was in that morning, the refrigerator and pantry were fully stocked, and all she needed to know for work Monday morning was on her home desk. Another quick hug and he and Will were gone.

Caroline stood alone in the middle of her luxurious apartment, the epitome of success and elegance. What was once her preferred place to be now felt strangely uncomfortable, a sterile, cold space. She wandered from room to room, feeling like a visitor in her own home. It was quiet, too quiet, so she opened the balcony doors, and the city's abrasive noises rushed in on her. Feeling assaulted, Caroline quickly shut them with a bang thinking, *this reentry is going to take some adjusting*. Putting her things away, she noticed the condition of her nails. They were perfect for gardening and wreath making, but not so much for meeting with advertising clients. Deciding to go for the works, she called down to the spa for a next-day appointment. *Maybe a few hours of pampering will help me realign.*

She went to press Otis on speed dial but stopped. The same for Emmy. It was too soon for her to mix the two worlds. This side of her life, the one Caroline had always strived for, flourished in, needed time to reinstate itself. Or not. At a loss for what to do next, Caroline sat down at her desk and dug into the files Hector had left. Her accounts, poorly managed in her absence (which had been her goal), were a disaster. They were in dire need of her expertise and client relationships to save them. She began strategizing how best to put out the multiple fires, making notes mentally and in the margins. By the time she rubbed her eyes and checked the clock, it was almost two in the morning. Caroline climbed into the unwelcoming, vacant bed and tried to fall asleep in the icy silence. A feeling of complete isolation replaced Otis's arms, Charlie's snoring, and nature's nighttime sounds. Sleep, when it finally came, was uneasy and fitful.

Caroline woke the following day and knew it was early. Not because of the sun's placement in her window or birds singing, but because of the harsh red digits that glared at her from the alarm clock. "Well, good morning to you too, you angry thing," she growled at it. The thought of drinking her coffee in the apartment's silent, climate-controlled environment was enough to send her to the coffee shop downstairs and out to the patch of green across the street. She got a kick out of Robert the doorman's double-take when she said good morning on her way out. Not only had he never seen Ms. McMerritt up so early, but she was wearing a ball cap and sweats, and heaven forbid, even gave him a friendly greeting!

Caroline forced herself to finish the coffee among pigeons pooping around her feet and the choking smell of exhaust replacing the coffee's aroma. This was a world away from the fresh air, filled with the scent of pine and chirping birds she had shared her summer mornings with. *I so miss my cardinal!* Heading back to the apartment, she saw a homeless man digging through a garbage can in front of her building. Caroline reached in her pocket and handed him a five-dollar bill, a first for her. *If I keep this up, poor Robert is going to need therapy.* The thought made her smile.

The spa treatment somewhat rejuvenated her, and she decided to reacquaint herself with the city that had enchanted her for so long. Taking along her best positive attitude, Caroline walked and took the subway to all her favorite spots: The Guggenheim Museum on 5th Avenue and Times Square, always full of hopeful dancers and actors, and the ever-present tourists. She ate lunch at the Loeb Boathouse in Central Park, walked across the iconic Brooklyn Bridge, bought a latte, and sat in Brooklyn Bridge Park admiring the Manhattan skyline while listening to families at play. She stopped by her favorite Thai restaurant to order takeout for dinner and the deli to pick up bagels for breakfast on the way home.

Back at the apartment, a tired Caroline admitted she'd enjoyed the day. But it was only one day. Could she ever embrace the frenetic movement and ever-present noise of the city again? Not to mention the smell and the thin coat of grim that overlaid everything, including her. At that thought, Caroline headed for the shower, wondering how she'd overlooked these things for so long, knowing the answer. Ambition. It was the city's heartbeat, its life's blood, and Caroline had needed it flowing through her veins to keep hers alive. Did she still? Only time would tell.

# Chapter XXVI

By seven-thirty the next morning. Caroline was downstairs, chatting with a pleasantly surprised Robert, while she waited for her car, two more firsts. Robert answered all her inquires. He was a retired cop, married almost forty-five years to his high school sweetheart, had three kids and eight grandchildren. When her driver pulled up and saw her waiting, he raced around the car to hold the door, apologizing profusely.

"Ms. McMerritt, an early pick-up wasn't on the schedule, and–" With a smile, Caroline waved her hand. "No worries, but I will be leaving for the office by seven-thirty moving forward."

As the driver shut the door, he gave Robert a startled look.

"Beats me what got into her, but let's enjoy it while it lasts," he said with a shrug.

They weren't the only ones taken aback by Caroline's uncharacteristic friendliness. She left a trail of gaping mouths from the receptionist whose outfit she complimented to the cubicles where she stopped to say a cheerful good morning. The final shock came to Hector when he discovered his sister-in-law already at her desk when he arrived.

"You're early, rested, and looking positively put together." Hector sniffed the air around her, "And no cigarette smoke or breath mints."

"I smoked because of stress, anger, and alcohol. Eliminate the causes, and it's easier to control the craving. Plus, it made me even more nauseous going through my divorce with Don Julio."

"So no more babysitting. Am I out of a job?"

Caroline rolled her eyes, "Don't tempt me. Now, get settled so we can get to work doing what you're really paid to do."

Hector gave a courtly bow and grinned. "Glad to see your tongue is as sharp as ever."

Maci came barging through the outer office five minutes later and stopped dead in her tracks when she saw her behind the desk. Caroline caught a flash of disappointment cross Maci's face before she regained her composure.

"I know how inconvenient and annoying it is for you, Maci, but, yes, I'm back as ordered."

Maci ignored her. "You've got thirty days to save the accounts you left floundering before I turn them over to someone else."

*So that's it.* "Ahhh, I see. You've already groomed someone to take my place. Someone much more pliable to your ways, I'm sure. Well, tell them they have a long wait. And I didn't abandon my accounts. On the contrary, you forced me to take a leave of absence."

"You refused to answer emails and calls to help us best serve your clients. That's abandonment."

"No, Maci, that's self-preservation. And by the looks of things, a brilliant move on my part. You should know better than to underestimate me. Tell your protégé better luck next time."

"Do your job, Caroline. No more chances." With that, Caroline's boss stormed out.

"Well, that's an ugly way to start the day," Hector pointed out. Caroline agreed but had expected it and was more eager than ever to get to work.

Maci had messed with the wrong lady.

Hector and his boss spent the morning prioritizing clients by the condition of their accounts. None were in good shape, but some were ready to walk. They divided the list in two, Caroline taking the most urgent and got on the phones to schmooze irate CEOs. By six o'clock, berated and chastised for hours, they'd managed to secure appointments with all but a few. Caroline would wine and dine those until she won them back. *I am nothing if not charming when wooing a company*, she assured herself. No one was better.

By the end of the month, Caroline had whittled away at her clients' discord by cajoling them with promises, flattery, fiend humbleness, and twenty-four-hour availability. Exhausted but triumphant, her objectives met, she could now relax and be more aware of her surroundings. So, she was surprised by Robert's cold "Morning Ma'am," and the driver immediately raising the car's partition without a word. When the receptionist didn't return her wave nor the cubicles her "Good Morning," Caroline knew something was amiss. She complained to Hector about everyone's frigid attitude, and he gave her a dumbfounded look.

"You honestly don't know, do you?"

"Know what?"

"When you're work-driven, you're like a racehorse; blinders on and only the finish line matters. If you acknowledge people at all, it's with impatience or aloofness."

"In other words, I'm a cold bitch."

"Yes, that sums it up perfectly, I'm afraid."

Had Caroline always realized how she acted towards others when consumed with her job and didn't care because she was obsessed with it? *Yes*, she acknowledged. For her, success had always meant perfection with no room for distractions. *Well, I care now.* And if maintaining her status as the best meant sacrificing even brief exchanges of pleasantries with others, she would change it. That no longer seemed an acceptable way to do life for her.

Her thoughts were interrupted by Maci summoning her to her office. *What now*, Caroline wondered, annoyed. She arrived to find Maci talking with a young Harvard type, handsome, oozing wealth and charm.

"Caroline, meet Chad. He finished his internship this summer, and PG&G was impressed enough to hire him. We'd like you to be his mentor, show him the ropes, introduce your accounts, etcetera."

Incensed but hardly stunned, Caroline shook his hand and immediately dismissed him. "I'd like to talk to Maci privately, Chad."

His confidence very much intact, he said, "Of course, I'll see you Monday," and strode out of the office.

Caroline pounced. "Don't insult my intelligence, Maci. I see this for exactly what it is, and I'm not playing!"

"You have no choice. Chad's daddy is on the board and has high expectations for him in this firm. Your clients are the biggest, so..."

"So, after busting my ass to save them, I'm expected to groom my replacement and put myself out of a job?"

"Don't be dramatic. We'll find some position for you here."

"Some position? So, the plan was to send me out on leave and replace me with boy wonder while I was gone. Except I screwed things up by going silent."

Maci shrugged. "You've been around the business long enough to know how it works, Caroline. You've had a nice ride;

it would be a shame for you to jump off too soon now. That will be all, see you on Monday." *Like hell, you will!*

Caroline stormed back to her office and grabbed her pocketbook. She stuffed the desktop Rolodex into her bag and, without a word to anyone, left the building, and hailed a cab. Once home, she immediately called downstairs to have a bottle of Don Julio sent up, and in a blind rage, stripped down and stood under an ice-cold shower until she could see straight. Caroline, never professionally one-upped, much less cast aside, felt like a loser for the first time in her career. She had lost and had no idea how to handle it. After throwing on a silk robe, she turned her phone off, and poured a shot from the delivered tequila bottle. Reverently Caroline set it down on the table and stared, hunger in her eyes, as if it were a forbidden lover. *It is a lover. A dangerous lover, a serpent of temptation,* her inner voice warned. She knew if she succumbed, there would be no turning back. Its toxic grip would wrap around her neck, choking the life out of her. And still, she lusted after it, craved its numbing touch. Time stood still as the battle of wills within her left each other bloodied and barely standing. With her sanity threatened and her strength drained, Caroline reached for the table, took her mother's journal, and began to read through her tears.

*It's our first year alone at the lake since Will was born. It's like being newlyweds but so much more. We have built a wonderful life together, shared so much, raised two beautiful children, and I now can reap the rewards of it all. Bill and I reminisce for hours, sometimes laughing, other times shedding a tear, but always grateful for our journey. We know how blessed we are that our love is more vital than ever before. So many couples lose sight of one another through the years and grow apart, or worse, harbor resentments over unspoken disappointments. We have always tackled life as a team and never wavered in our commitment. I only hope our children can find such a rare gift, recognize it, grab hold of and cherish it.*

*I shared this thought with Bill as I gardened, and he worked on the old truck. Always pragmatic, my husband offered this analogy: Will and Caroline were tiny seeds planted in the richest soil we could find. We nurtured, fed, and watered them until they grew into robust, mature plants that could stand independently. I agreed but confessed I was still worried about them. Would Will find a loving partner who appreciated his gentle heart and trusting nature, not take advantage of him? Could he make a decent living on his art, as he dreams? And Caroline's endless ambition and single-mindedness. Would she ever use them for more than career and success? Eventually, come to understand those attributes can contribute to personal growth and happiness as well? Will our daughter ever find her life balance? He came over, kissed me gently, and said, "They grew up in a garden of respect, love, and fairness. They know how to do it right. Our children are resilient Meri and will bloom wherever planted. They will be fine." And just like that, my mind was eased. What a wonderful best friend I have in my husband.*

That was her mother's final entry in the journal. The accident took her parents' lives later that year.

As Caroline closed the book, she found her eyes drawn to the balcony, not the shot glass. On the railing, high above the city, stood a cardinal on one foot. *Balance.* Laughing and crying much different tears, she went to the window to blow it a kiss. The bird lowered its foot, cocked its head, and flew away.

Caroline threw some clothes on, rushed through the lobby and into a cab. Three hours later, she pulled up in her new pick-up truck and asked a stunned Robert to have it valeted. She hastily packed some boxes with the surprisingly few things she wanted to keep, threw some essentials in a suitcase, and called downstairs for help loading the truck. After a quick, final sweep-through, Caroline closed and locked the door to the apartment and her city life. She was done treading water; it was time to swim.

The shot of tequila stood alone, untouched on the coffee table. Defeated by an Amazon Queen and a little red bird.

Caroline called Will and Hector on the way to Maine. Will was angry she had turned her phone off but softened when he heard the battle she had fought and won. They were both ecstatic over her decision, and after a brief celebration, had some questions.

Had she told PG&G? "No. I will send them an email Monday morning. After what they pulled, they deserved nothing more."

“Love it!,” Hector exclaimed. “Are we stealing some clients too?”

“Not yet. My contract has a non-compete clause. But I did grab my Rolodex on the way out. Proof that outdated methods still have their place.”

She laughed when Hector told her he was so proud. “You never disappoint,” he said and asked about the apartment.

"It's all yours, bro-in-law, as is the furniture. I took what I wanted. Please sell the rest and donate the proceeds to a charity. Google Addisen Family nonprofits and pick one. "

What would she do now to satisfy her ever-present drive? “I hope to invest my time and money into a garden design business with Emmy. It was always a dream of hers, but startup money was a problem. With that solved, perhaps she’s willing to give it a go with a partner.”

Will, ever the overprotective brother, told her to expect him and Hector the following weekend. It was time for him to check out this Otis guy a little more carefully. Caroline squawked, but just a little. She loved when Will looked out for her. Blowing kisses into the phone, Caroline hung up and finished her journey in contented silence. Arriving well past midnight, she dragged only the suitcase in, dropped on the bed fully clothed, and fell into the deep sleep of a carefree child.

Caroline contently smiled as she woke to the sound of nature, ushering in the promise of her day to come. Full of energy she bounced out of bed and went down to make a special breakfast. After placing a mug of black coffee and slices of peanut butter toast at the end of the dock, she took her own coffee to the porch swing. The cardinal landed on the railing in a show of support, and they sat in excited anticipation together. They didn't have to wait long. As was its habit, the boat slowed as it passed her cabin. Seeing breakfast on the dock, Otis cut the engine. "Well, I'll be damned," he said to Charlie. Grabbing his mug, he walked to the porch, never taking his eyes off Caroline, as if afraid she would disappear again. "It's black, just how you like it," she whispered. Otis swallowed her whole in a hug while Charlie smothered them in peanut butter kisses.

Caroline was home.

# Epilogue

Caroline's Journal

*This is the first of many entries, a way to reach my future children, as Mom did me. My goal is to reveal a private, unseen piece of me. My inner thoughts, feelings, experiences, and fears. Shared bits of wisdom, honesty, love. To articulate with the written word, the guidance my mother's diary provided me, along with my own insights I've picked up along the way. I only hope I can be as graceful and potent as she.*

---

*So much has happened this year, I don't know where to begin…*

*I never unloaded my truck at the cabin. After two days of hibernation there together, Otis and I drove it to his place, and that was that. We haven't spent a night apart since. We moved my parent's easy chair, rocker, and bookshelves, along with his mom's reading nook, to a guest room and created a family library of sorts. We spend some evenings reading there, surrounded by our parents' memories. It's my favorite room in the house. (Well, maybe my second.) Mom's hope chest sits at the foot of our bed, with her journal tucked in the very spot I found it. It has, quite simply, saved my life, and I need it near my dreams.*

*Emmy was over the moon at the idea of starting a business together, and it turns out we're quite the team. Cardinal Garden Designs has enough work to maintain a sizeable staff and will soon need more. We're in Maine and New Hampshire now, but my goal is to have us throughout New England in a year or two. That will give us enough capital to open our own nursery. The gardens around my parent's cabin have matured beautifully, making it the perfect location for a garden design company. Worktables, to layout design blueprints, now line the living area, and the upstairs loft serves as our office. What used to be my parent's bedroom is a display room for our custom-designed wreaths.*

*I still haven't decided what to do about the advertising business. There's no rush; I have time to contemplate. I stay in touch with some clients, careful not to overstep any legal boundaries. I'm reasonably confident they would come with me should I choose to get back into the rat race, but I'm not certain I will. Right now, I'm perfectly content having one client, Cardinal. I thrive on creating ad campaigns, promotions, and marketing strategies for our business's growth, and, for now, it more than satisfies my drive. Will it always? Time will tell…*

*Will and Hector are frequent visitors and have developed strong friendships with Otis, Emmy, and Dan. I still have trouble keeping a straight face seeing my brother-in-law try to pull off a flannel shirt and jeans but give him credit for trying. Hector went into PG&G the Monday I sent my resignation and quit. He refused to be a party to my replacement's success. Instead, he bought into a gourmet coffee shop in Risedale and is trying to master the art of coffee making. Otis, quick to see how sharp Hector is and his love of the city, hired him to represent his grandfather's estate on the boards of the non-profits. As a result, Otis can concentrate on his beloved Addisen, and Hector gets to dress up and get his NYC fix on occasion. It's a win-win all around. According to Will, he's a much better overseer than a barista, thank goodness.*

*Honoring tradition, we have started a once-a-month 'Saturday Time' that Will and Hector rarely miss. Addisen's various managers and their families join our inner circle for a potluck, s'mores, and plenty of good times around the fire. The mayor, of course, is always the center of attention. Oh, how I love my community and being a part of Addisen pride!*

*Speaking of pride…I am still sober and intend to stay that way. I rarely think about alcohol now, even when around others drinking. Is it because I eliminated all that drove me to it? Or, because my life is more balanced? I don't know. But I do know better than to test it. Ever.*

*Dad was right. A hardy flower can bloom wherever planted. But to thrive, it needs more than a crack in the sidewalk. It needs space to grow, to be watered with love, and able to hold its face to the unfiltered sun. I'm living proof of that. I believe fate brought me here for my mother to teach me this very truth.*

*Many years ago, Mom intuited her young daughter's path would be different from her own. She had supported me down my chosen lane, but when it led me to a cliff's edge, she had me brought back home to nurture me once again. To help me heal. Her words led me to embrace the unequivocal gift of loving and being loved by a good man and the value of a close friend. They gave me an appreciation for nature and showed me the importance of tradition. I need to find a different path now, one to accommodate both some of the old and the new me. A daunting task, to be sure, but I've finally learned the lesson Mom spent a lifetime trying to teach me: patience. Baby steps…*

*I made a wreath for our front door a while back. Dried Speedwell encompasses the inner circle, their blue blossoms representing the lake. I collected nature's treasures from the lake's different amenities to honor each generation's contribution to the family legacy. As with Emmy's, I added a nest to portray our home but wove a red ribbon through ours to acknowledge the cardinals, our family members, who surround us with protection and love.*

*This morning I tucked an egg into the nest with a mixture of sheer joy and wonder pumping from my heart and pulsing through my veins. Tonight, I will show Otis.*

*As I write this, my cardinal touches down to join me and hops around in excitement, elated. I'm not the least bit surprised. After all, mothers always seem to know…*

# About the Author

Belle A. DeCosta's memoir, *Echoes in the Mirror*, was published in June 2020, and her piece, "An Introduction," is featured in the 2020 ARIA Anthology, *Hope*.

Belle is the creator and director of Tap N Time, a seated tap and rhythm class designed for the elderly. When not traveling to nursing homes to share her program, she enjoys her grandson, being in nature, dining with friends, and writing.

Belle shares a home in East Providence, RI, with her beloved hound, J.D., and an aquarium full of assorted fish.

Made in the USA
Middletown, DE
16 August 2023

36737279R00109